DEEDS NOT WORDS

A FAMILY DIVIDED

KAY RACE

Kay Race

October 2022

For Keith, my rock, the love and light of my life.

"Better broken windows than broken promises."

Mrs Emmeline Pankhurst

1912

AUTHOR'S NOTE

It is important to note that there is a distinction between "suffragists" and "suffragettes". The former believed in using constitutional methods in pursuit of the women's franchise whilst the latter, under the leadership of Mrs Emmeline Pankhurst and her daughters, believed that direct action was necessary to achieve this goal, hence their slogan: "Deeds not words".

FOREWORD

This, the third book in the Frobisher Family Saga, follows events from 1909 until the beginning of the First World War. This is a period during which Mrs Pankhurst and the members of the Women's Social and Political Union had come to the decision that peaceful methods were not achieving their goal of securing votes for women.

They embarked on a campaign of direct action which began with disrupting political meetings, and progressed to the height of their escalating militancy when they started fires, sent letter bombs (which they invented) and planted explosives in buildings.

Throughout this time imprisoned suffragettes went on hunger strike and suffered repeated force-feeding which was nothing less than a brutal and legalised form of torture and violence against women.

I have exercised some artistic licence in respect of certain incidents, bringing them forward by a couple of years or so, to fit into the timeframe of this book, e.g. the portrait of King George V was slashed by Maude Edwards in 1914. However other events, including "Black Friday" and the

Women's Coronation Procession are accurate and based on actual people, dates and places. I have included some historical characters alongside my own fictitious ones.

For those readers who are unfamiliar with Edinburgh, you may, perhaps, want to refer to a street map of the city for a deeper appreciation of the simultaneous activities that take place in chapter 33.

A glossary of Scots words can be found at the back of the book. I hope you enjoy catching up with old friends from my previous novels, and meeting new ones in this book.

Kay Race

October 2022

ALSO BY KAY RACE

Trapped in the Dark Decade

November 2018

Book 1 in the Dark Edinburgh Series

Dark Past, Secret Present

October 2020

Book 2 in the Dark Edinburgh Series

Dark Hearts, Enlightened Souls

May 2021

Book 3 in the Dark Edinburgh Series

Against the Odds

November 2021

Book 1 in the Frobisher Family Saga

Into the Fray

May 2022

Book 2 in the Frobisher Family Saga

1

EDINBURGH

5TH NOVEMBER 1909 2AM

I t was a cold and dark moonless night in the city of Edinburgh. Two figures, dressed in dark clothes, hurried furtively along the north side of Charlotte Square. Over a number of nights, they had monitored the movements of the bobby on the beat and knew that they had a seven-minute window of opportunity to reach their target and complete the task assigned to them.

They stopped when they reached number 6 and looked about to make sure they were alone and unobserved before ascending the steps to the large front door.

"Have you got the can and the rag ready?" asked one, in a whisper, while shining a torch on the letterbox.

"Aye," replied the other, taking the items out of a jute bag, "hold the letterbox open while I feed the cloth through."

Wearing protective rubber gloves, they quickly fed the length of oil-soaked rag through the large brass opening, leaving enough of it on the outside to set it alight.

"Pour the remainder of the oil through," said the first

person, taking matches out of a coat pocket. "Stand well back!" the other urged, as the match was struck.

In the still cold of the early morning, the sound of the match striking seemed ominously loud and, although they knew the house was not occupied, they feared someone in the neighbouring houses would hear and they'd be discovered before they could finish the job.

Quickly, with deft movements, the lighted match was put to the end of the rag and it ignited immediately. Eager flames began to lick up and down the door as the cloth on the inside of the letterbox quickly caught fire.

For a fraction of a second both froze at the sight of the gathering conflagration before the first one said in hoarse whisper "Run!" As the other figure bent to pick up the the can and bag, the first added urgently, "Leave the damn thing and move!"

Both fled down the steps and along the still empty Square. Just as they turned into North Charlotte Street they heard the shrill blast of a police whistle and they disappeared like shadows into the dark backstreets of the New Town.

2

4 HATTON PLACE

FRIDAY 5TH NOVEMBER 1909

Sir Charles and Lady Frobisher were just finishing breakfast when Maggie, their housekeeper, brought in the morning newspaper. Charles had been knighted in 1905 for his services to paediatric medicine and in 1906 he became the Liberal Member of Parliament for the Edinburgh South seat, ousting the sitting Liberal Unionist candidate.

"Your *Scotsman* Sir Charles, Ah'm afraid the paper laddie wis a bit late this mornin'. Ah ken ye like tae read it wi' yer breakfast. He says he slept in," said Maggie, who was prone to making any statement longer than was necessary. The Frobishers, who were well used to Maggie's streams of consciousness, exchanged smiles.

Still smiling, Sir Charles said, "Thank you Maggie, I'll read it with my coffee."

Lady Frobisher added, "You may clear the table Maggie, but leave the tea and coffee pots."

"Yes Lady Frobisher," she replied and quickly removed the breakfast dishes.

Maggie had just closed the door behind her when

Charles unfolded the paper, crying out, "Good God Louisa! Look at this!"

Louisa hurried around the table and read the headlines that had shocked Charles so. The article read as follows:

"ARSON ATTACK ON HOUSE OF SECRETARY OF STATE FOR SCOTLAND

Just after 2 a.m. this morning, Constable McVicar, who was patrolling his beat at the West End, spotted flames and smoke pouring from the ground floor of Bute House, the official home of the Secretary of State for Scotland. By good chance, the Scottish Secretary, Sir John Sinclair and his family were not on the premises and the domestic staff, who had been asleep on the top floor and had been awakened by the breaking of glass due to the heat of the blaze, managed to escape via the back staircase to the safety of the Mews. Fortunately, no one was harmed in the incident. The constable alerted the Fire Brigade, who arrived within seven minutes and they were able to extinguish the fire, saving the house from burning down. Fire Chief, Robert Duncanson, told the *Scotsman*, after an examination of the premises,

"This fire was started deliberately, with highly flammable fluid which had been poured through the letterbox of the front door. We found an oil can and a bag on the doorstep and a postcard with the words "Votes for women" written on it.

The police are investigating this as an arson attack and are conducting interviews with residents of the Square in the hope that somebody saw the culprit, or culprits, who perpetrated this terrible act. We will keep our readers informed of further developments, but it is believed that the Secretary of State's home was a target because of his favourable stance on force-feeding of hunger-striking suffragettes in Scottish prisons, although as yet, unlike English prisons who have been using forcible feeding for the past two years, it has not been implemented in Scotland."

"THANK God John and his family were in London, the alternative doesn't bear thinking about," Charles said.

"Oh Charles, how awful!" Louisa exclaimed, when she had finished reading the article. A thought suddenly struck her and she added, "You don't think Evangeline could possibly have had anything to do with it, do you?"

Without waiting for a reply, she hurried out of the room and up the stairs. On opening the door to her daughter's bedroom she froze. The bed had not been slept in. She returned to the morning room, looking very worried now.

"What is it Louisa?" asked Charles, folding the paper and laying it on the table, his appetite for the morning's news having evaporated.

"It's Evangeline," said Louisa, her hand at her throat, "she's not in her room and her bed hasn't been slept in. Wherever can she be?"

Just at that moment the telephone in the hall rang and they heard Maggie answering it. A moment later she came into the room and announced, "Lady Moncrieff is on the telephone Lady Frobisher." Lady Moncrieff was Louisa's mother.

She picked up the instrument and said, "Good morning Mother, how are you?"

"Louisa my dear, I'm just ringing to let you know that Evangeline is here, I didn't want you worrying when you discovered that she wasn't at home. She must have come in after we had gone to bed and she brought a friend with her."

"Oh Mother," she said, relief flooding through her, "I've just been up to her bedroom and saw that she hadn't come home last night. Thank you for letting us know and putting our minds at rest."

Evangeline had been given a key to her grandparents house in Heriot Row and she would sometimes stay there if she was at a meeting in that part of town, rather than take a hackney cab to the south side of the city.

Louisa put the telephone down thoughtfully and went back into the morning room to tell Charles the good news.

Charles, who had been listening to Louisa's end of the conversation, asked, "She stayed with your parents last night? Did your mother say what time she arrived?"

Chewing her bottom lip, always a sign that Louisa was unsure or anxious, she replied, "That's just it Charles, Mother said she must have arrived after they'd gone to bed."

Charles looked at the newspaper again and frowned. "You do realise that Charlotte Square is not very far from your parents house, it being at the west end of Heriot Row?"

Louisa sat down heavily, her legs feeling too weak to stand, as the meaning of her husband's words sank in.

Her hand at her throat again, she said, "Charles you can't possibly believe that Evangeline would set fire to someone's home? Throwing eggs at Mr Churchill is one thing, but setting a house on fire is another thing altogether."

Evangeline had been arrested in Dundee in May 1908 for throwing eggs at Winston Churchill while he was campaigning as a Liberal candidate in the by-election there. She was charged with Breach of the Peace and assault and sentenced to a fine of two pounds or ten days in prison. She refused to pay the fine and was released after 3 days on hunger strike.

Charles put his head in his hands. After a few moments pause he looked at Louisa and said, "Louisa my dear, I do not want to think that our only child would do such a thing, but ever since you brought her back from the "Mud March" in London two and a half years ago, she has been particularly single-minded and determined to carry out the wishes of those blasted Pankhurst women."

They both cast their minds back to the time when Evangeline, at the age of twenty, announced to her parents that she was leaving the Edinburgh Women's Suffrage Society (EWSS) and joining Mrs Pankhurst's Women's Social and Political Union (WSPU).

She had told them, "Mother, you, Letty and both my grandmothers know that four decades of petitions and processions have failed to get women the vote and I agree with Mrs Pankhurst, we have to make the politicians listen to us. If we simply march in a ladylike fashion, being seen but not heard then nothing will change. If we keep doing the same thing, we'll keep getting the same result - and that is no vote." She had stormed out of the room saying, "I'm joining Mrs Pankhurst's suffragettes first thing tomorrow."

"I wish I had never taken her to that march, but it was organised by us, or at least the National Union of Women's Suffrage Societies (NUWSS), I didn't know there would be any suffragettes there. As soon as she spotted Christabel Pankhurst, she talked of nothing else. Oh Charles," she almost wailed, "what are we going to do with her?"

"I don't know Louisa," he said, shaking his head again, "but I know what we should have done. We should have been more strict and not let her have her own way as much as we did."

"She was always a strong-willed child, but I thought she would grow out of it, be a little compliant at times. Even Letty, who used to be have such a positive influence on her, hasn't been able to get through to her lately."

Letty, Charles's sister and Louisa's best friend, had become a doctor when women were banned from medical training in the United Kingdom and, against the odds, she and five companions left home and loved ones to study medicine in Dublin. Letty currently ran an Edinburgh medical practice with her husband, Dr Wilf Cunningham.

"Yes, I know," said Louisa. "Letty has been such a good role model and she feels she's failed Evangeline both as an aunt and a godmother. You know what I think is worse than anything?"

"What is that my dear?"asked Charles.

"Dropping out of medical school to be a full time WSPU member after everything Letty had to do to become a doctor." she replied.

"I know," Charles agreed. "It's something I often think about. She's had it all handed to her on a plate and she's just thrown it away." He got up from the table and kissed Louisa. "I'm going to my constituency office now, if Evangeline comes home while I'm out tell her we both need to talk to her this evening. I don't care what plans she has, she has to be at home this evening."

"Alright Charles, I'll try to get her to be here. Have a good day."

3

39 HERIOT ROW

MUCH EARLIER THAT DAY

E vangeline Frobisher let herself and Jessie Gilhooley into the Georgian house in Heriot Row. Her maternal grandparents, Lord and Lady Moncrieff, had always indulged their only grandchild and it hadn't taken much for her to convince them to let her have a key to their house. She'd argued that it was more convenient and, possibly safer, for her to stay there when she was at a late meeting in that area of the city. Evangeline had her own room there since she'd been a child and had often stayed overnight when her mother and father went out socially.

Even though her grandmother disapproved of her joining the militant WSPU, she wanted to keep her granddaughter placated in the hope that being a suffragette was just a phase, as she was still young at twenty-two. Lady Moncrieff, who had been a suffragist since 1867 and had spent several years being the chairwoman of the EWSS, believed in women getting the vote through constitutional means and, like her daughter Louisa, was strongly opposed to the violent methods advocated and sanctioned by the Pankhursts.

As the two women entered the house silently, Evangeline said, "Come down to the kitchen and we'll get something to eat and drink."

Jessie followed her down the back stairs and into the large basement kitchen and switched on the electric light. The house had been completely electrified a few years previously, as had her own home in Hatton Place.

"Sit down," she said, pointing to the huge scrubbed pine table which was surrounded by 8 sturdy chairs, "and I'll make us sandwiches and a pot of tea." Jessie did as she was told and Evangeline went on, "I don't know about you Jessie, but I'm famished, these missions always give me an appetite."

"Me as well," said Jessie who was now a full-time paid organiser of the Edinburgh branch of the WSPU. She had gladly left her job as a typesetter with the Riverside Press when she'd been offered better paid work with the WSPU.

Evangeline put a plate of ham sandwiches down in front of Jessie and then poured tea for them both. Stifling a yawn, she said, "Well, we did the best we could Jessie, but I suspect the blaze was put out before it could do too much damage."

"Aye," agreed Jessie, munching hungrily on her sandwich, "but it's a shot across the bow for John Sinclair. Ah'll never forgive him for trying to introduce that torture intae Scottish prisons.

"I'd like to do the same to those brutal doctors in English gaols. Imagine forcing a thick rubber tube up some poor woman's nose as she's being held down by God knows how many wardresses!" said Evangeline, her anger rising as it always did when on this particular topic. "It's nothing more than legalised torture. What happened to "First do no harm?" It really makes my blood boil Jessie."

Both women fell silent for a few minutes, each thinking

about their fellow WSPU members enduring such barbaric treatment at the hands of the prison authorities and prison doctors in England.

The kitchen clock struck three o'clock and, coming out of her reverie, Evangeline said, "Time for bed, I'm exhausted. We'll find out about the extent of the damage in tomorrow's newspapers, no doubt."

After the adrenalin rush of setting the fire and their flight to Heriot Row, Jessie wearily hauled herself from the chair and asked, "What about the dishes Evangeline? We cannae leave them there," and she began to collect the plates and cups.

"Leave them in the sink Jessie, the housekeeper will see to them in the morning," was the reply.

DESPITE THEIR LATE NIGHT, Evangeline and Jessie were up and dressed for breakfast reasonably early next morning. Her grandmother was still in the morning room, having a second cup of tea. She looked up, surprised, when the young women came into the room.

"Evangeline, my dear," she said, "I had no idea you were here."

Evangeline dutifully kissed her on the cheek and said, "Good morning Grandmama, this is my friend Jessie Gilhooley and we were both at a late meeting last night at Florence McVie's house in Melville Place and didn't want to go all the way home. I hope it was alright to invite Jessie to stay?"

Lady Moncrieff said, with a warm smile, "Of course it's alright, you know your friends are always welcome Evangeline." She turned to Jessie and said, "Good morning Jessie, it's good to meet you."

"Thank you Lady Moncrieff," said Jessie shyly.

"What time did you get in? I didn't hear you come in." she said.

"Oh, it was about midnight Grandmama," Evangeline replied, looking her grandmother in the eye. She was becoming very adept at lying, she thought to herself.

"Does your mother know you're here dear?" she asked, wiping her mouth with a linen napkin.

"No, Grandmama, it was too late to telephone them from Florence's," she lied again.

"Very well, help yourself to breakfast and I shall telephone Louisa immediately so she doesn't worry when she realises that you're not at home."

"Thank you Grandmama, you're very thoughtful," Evangeline replied.

Just as she got to the door she stopped, thoughtful, then asked, "What about you Jessie, do you wish to call home?"

"We don't have a telephone, but thank you for the offer Lady Moncrieff."

She nodded and went into the hall to call her daughter. Evangeline and Jessie gave each other meaningful looks and set about putting food on plates and pouring tea.

4

5 TRON SQUARE, EDINBURGH

LATER THAT MORNING

J essie let herself into the small, but immaculately kept, flat situated just off the High Street. She knew she would have to have a good story prepared for when her husband came home from work in order to explain why she had not come home last night. She had decided the one that Evangeline had told her grandmother was as good as any and decided to go with that.

She walked into the small bedroom to change her clothes before going into the WSPU office and stopped short. Her husband was waiting for her and he did not look pleased.

"Bob?" she said, startled. "I thought you'd have gone tae work ages ago."

Robert Gilhooley was an inspector on the Edinburgh trams and always worked day shifts from 6am to 2pm.

"Where have you been all night?" he asked, barely controlling the rage that had been building up since his alarm went off at 5am and he realised Jessie hadn't come home from her suffragette meeting.

"The meeting went on longer than I thought so I stayed

at Evangeline's grandparents' house in Heriot Row," she said, then added placatingly, "Bob, you knew when I took this job that it involved evening work."

"Aye, *evening* work is one thing," he said, "but staying oot a' night is quite a different thing a'thegither. Now tell me the truth, ye've been wi' a man, haven't ye?" he said, towering over her. "Was it ane o' thae poncey men that think women should be allowed tae vote?" He lowered his face to hers and added in a menacing tone, "Well, wis it, eh?"

Jessie had never seen this side of her husband before and it frightened her.

"Ah've a'ready tellt ye Bob Gilhooley, Ah wis at a meetin' until midnight at the West End and Evangeline invited me tae stay at her granny's hoose so Ah didnae have tae walk a' the way hame in the dark oan ma ain." She dodged from under his glaring face and started to take her clothes out of the wardrobe, so she didn't see the blow coming. The next thing she knew was his fist hitting her in the eye and she fell to the floor, still clutching the blouse she'd just taken out of the wardrobe, and lost consciousness.

After a few moments, she came to and Bob was standing over her. "Ah'm gon tae work, Ah've a'ready lost three hours pay because o' you. Hoor!" he spat the obscenity at her and slammed out of the house.

Jessie hauled herself off the floor and sat on the bed feeling totally stunned by her husband's behaviour. She could feel her right eye swelling and she walked unsteadily through to the small scullery to put on a cold compress to try to reduce the damage caused by the vicious blow.

As she sat at the table, she thought about Bob and she suddenly realised that he must have resented her involvement in the WSPU for some time, although he had enjoyed the extra money she brought in. He'd obviously not minded her being a member of the EWSS which he'd apparently regarded as harmless, she reflected.

His words of warning, uttered many months previously, came back to her: "Ye're gonae get yersel' in serious trouble Jessie, if ye join in wi' their criminal acts," he'd said, shaking his head. "Throwin' eggs at members o' parlyment, or attackin' them wi' whips are crimes. Ah dinnae want ma wife comin' up before a sheriff an' bein' sent tae gaol. Dae ye hear me?"

So, to keep the peace, she had promised him that she would only be involved in the organisational aspects of the movement. She had lied, of course, she reflected now, as she'd been more than happy to set fire to pillar boxes and to break windows. Last night's activity had taken it that step further. She knew that trying to burn down a house was a serious crime. "But so is the brutal way the hunger-striking suffragettes in English prisons are treated," she told herself, justifying what she and Evangeline had done in Charlotte Square.

Coming back to the present, she put down the cold compress that she'd been holding to her eye for the past twenty minutes, went into the bedroom and looked at herself in the mirror. She touched her face gingerly. "Ow!" she cried out loud. Her eye was almost shut with the swelling and she decided she would have to wear a hat with a veil. "It's high time ye went intae the office," she said, to her reflection.

Twenty minutes later, Jessie was walking up the High Street and, as she turned into South Bridge, she saw "Bute House saved from total destruction by the actions of a quick-thinking bobby" on a news vendor's stand.

"We feared as much," she thought to herself as she continued up South Bridge and turned left along Drummond Street to the main door of the Victorian terraced house which provided the Edinburgh branch of the WSPU with spacious office accommodation.

The main office, where three women were busily typing, looked out over the street and Jessie had a similar office at the back of the house where she communicated with headquarters in London and the other Scottish branches. Evangeline had her own office on the first floor.

There was a fair-sized conference room opposite Jessie's office where the members met and strategies were discussed. It was in this room that the details of last month's Women's Social and Political Union Big March were planned and finalised - right down to the procession being led by Flora "The General" Drummond on horseback, carrying a banner which read:

To Mr Asquith,
Ye mauna tramp on the scotch thistle laddie!"

Another banner read:

"A guid cause maks a strong arm!"

And yet another:

"What's guid for John,
is guid for Janet!"

Several thousands of women, as well as many men, had taken part in the Procession which started in Bruntsfield Place, then down Lothian Road and along Princes Street where Mrs Pankhurst addressed an audience of four to five thousand in the Waverley Market.

. . .

JESSIE WENT into the front office and took off her hat and coat. Evangeline, who had been giving instructions to one of the secretaries, turned around. "Jessie, what on earth has happened to your eye?" she gasped. Addressing one of the women who were typing, she said, "Mary, make Jessie a cup of tea and bring it to her office." The three women seemed to have frozen in their chairs at the sight of Jessie's almost closed eye. Evangeline spoke more sharply this time, "Mary, tea please, and make it sweet and milky." at which Mary hurried out to the kitchen to do as she was asked.

"Come along to your office now Jessie dear," she said gently, "and let me examine your eye." She carefully examined Jessie's injured eye and said, "It won't need stitches but you'd better go to the Royal Infirmary for an X-ray to check your cheekbone isn't fractured."

Just then, Mary brought in the tea and Jessie thanked her and sipped at the hot drink. Even moving her lips gently caused pain to her whole face.

"How did you come by this injury Jessie?" Evangeline asked.

When Jessie told Evangeline about Bob and his suspicions, she became very angry. "What right has he got to assault you? He's nothing but a bully," she said hotly, "I'm going to give him a piece my mind and tell him you were with me."

"No, please don't Evangeline," Jessie begged her friend, "that would only make things worse. Things havnae been very good since Ah changed ma allegiance from the NUWSS to the WSPU, only Ah wis so busy that Ah hadnae realised how much he resented ma involvement here; no' until this mornin' that is."

"Has he ever done anything like this before?" Evangeline asked.

"No, but then Ah've never stayed oot a' night before either."

"Well that's no justification for attacking you, there are too many men in this society only too eager to use their hands on their wives. It's alright Jessie," Evangeline said after a few moments thought, "I won't say anything to him, but you must not go back home. Now that he's stepped across that line, he'll just find it easier to strike you again."

"But Ah've got nowhere to go Evangeline and he is ma husband," Jessie replied, at a loss to know what would be the best course of action.

"Stay in the apartment upstairs in the meantime, until we can find something more permanent."

"If yer sure it winnae be needed for any visitors," Jessie began, "it might be a good idea for Bob an' me tae be apart for a while."

"We've no visiting dignitaries expected until early next year so once we've been to the hospital, I'll go with you to fetch your belongings."

Fortunately Bob's blow to Jessie's face had not broken any bones, although her eye had totally closed. She was discharged with instructions to bathe it regularly with cold water or cold tea to reduce the swelling and told that the pain and bruising should subside within a week.

Evangeline hailed a cab to take Jessie home and the driver was instructed to wait for them. She helped Jessie pack a case with everything she would need for the next couple of weeks and on the way back to Drummond Street, she said, "I was all ready when you came into the office this morning, to have a post mortem of last night's mission when I saw the state you were in. If you feel up to it, we can do it when we get back. I asked Mary to get some newspapers so we can read a full account of what happened after we left the scene."

"That's fine by me," replied Jessie, adding, with the ghost of a smile, as her face was so sore, "Ah could dae wi' another cup o' tea though, but wi' nae sugar in it this time."

Evangeline gently squeezed Jessie's hand in solidarity as the cab travelled up South Bridge and stopped outside number 3 Drummond Street.

5

SALISBURY MEDICAL PRACTICE,

5TH NOVEMBER 1909

About a mile to the south of the WSPU office, Drs Wilf and Letty Cunningham and Rose Buchan were having lunch in the kitchen of the Salisbury Medical Practice. Not surprisingly, the conversation focused on the attempted arson attack on the Secretary for Scotland's house in Charlotte Square.

"Oh my goodness!" exclaimed Rose, after reading the report in the *Scotsman* "how fortunate that there was nobody on the lower floors. It says here," she quoted from the paper:

"The domestic staff, whose accommodation is on the attic floor, were wakened by the breaking of glass and made their escape down the back stairs, through the back basement door and to safety in the Mews."

Wilf shook his head and said, "I fear to think of the loss of life if it had happened when the family were at home."

Letty, who had been silent until now, spoke solemnly, "I think the time was chosen deliberately Wilf."

"What do you mean Letty?" he asked.

"The pattern of suffragette arson attacks throughout the

country so far, has been on property belonging to members of the government when the residents have not been at home," she replied.

Rose's eyes widened in shock as a thought struck her and she asked, "Dr Letty, you don't think Miss Evangeline had anything to do with it, do you?"

Rose, who had once been a maid in Letty's parents' household could still not bring herself to call people, who she regarded as her "betters" by their first name only, despite having been told to do so on many occasions over the years.

"I don't know Rose, but I do know that my niece is totally in thrall to the Pankhurst women, so I suppose it is possible," she said, "although I would prefer to think otherwise and that she had nothing to do with it."

"They really are going too far," said Wilf, who had been a supporter of women's suffrage for a few decades now and was a member of the Men's League for Women's Suffrage, "Perhaps constitutional methods aren't getting you the vote, but breaking the law and risking lives is beyond the pale, as far as I'm concerned."

"I can, in a way, see their point," said Rose tentatively.

Both Wilf and Letty looked at her in disbelief. "Rose, you surely can't be thinking of joining the Women's Social and Political Union too?" asked a shocked Letty.

"No, of course not, but I can see that after years, no, decades of peaceful campaigning, marches and petitioning members of parliament and we still don't have the vote, that it obviously seems to the many who have joined the WSPU that if we keep doing the same things that we've always done, nothing will change."

"Go on," said Wilf, interested, and inwardly pleased, to see Rose so confident now, after the struggle to recover from terrible abuse in the white slave trade when she was only a child.

"It seems to me," she said, taking a deep breath and unconsciously straightening her shoulders, "being peaceful and ladylike is not leading us any closer to getting the vote. How many Bills have been presented to Parliament and failed for one reason or another?"

"Yes," said Wilf, "but each time there are more MP's in favour of female enfranchisement."

"Yet it still hasn't got us the vote," Rose replied. "Do you realise that five Bills introduced to the House of Commons have failed? What does that say about our supposed supporters inside parliament?"

Wilf held his hands up in a gesture of surrender. "Alright Rose, I concede your point that all of that has not resulted in the vote being extended to women, so go on with what you were saying about seeing their point," encouraged Wilf.

"I totally disagree with the suffragettes' campaign of militancy, but it seems clear that after fifty years of peaceful campaigning, we are no further forward than when John Stuart Mill presented the first mass petition to parliament in 1867," said Rose, to which Letty and Wilf nodded. "Now that makes me think that those methods are not effective."

"Yes," said Wilf, "but you surely don't think attacking members of the government and setting fire to their property is going to get them the vote either?"

"No, I personally don't think it will, but the publicity they're getting from their actions is bringing the question of votes for women into the public mind," said Rose, warming to her theme now, and Letty smiled, as amazed at the transformation in Rose over the years as Wilf was, and she felt very proud of their "little Rose".

"Well," she continued, "they're getting attention every

single day, not just on occasional procession and march days."

"I can see what you're saying about the lack of progress from peaceful campaigning and that you don't approve of, or agree with, what the suffragettes are doing, but where does that leave you and me Rose?" asked Letty, puzzled and a little frustrated.

"It leaves us with the Women's Freedom League," replied Rose. "I've been thinking of joining them and wondered whether you might want to join with me."

Letty looked at Wilf doubtfully, biting her lower lip which was always a sign of turmoil or agitation.

"I don't know Rose," she said hesitantly, not wanting to commit herself either way.

"Think about it Dr Letty," Rose said, "but just bear in mind that they advocate non-violent protest, which is one of the reasons why many left the Pankhursts' organisation; that and the fact that it wasn't and isn't being run democratically since Mrs Pankhurst and her daughter, Christabel, make the rules and keep a tight control over the running of their campaigns."

The Women's Freedom League (WFL) had been founded two years previously. A number of women left when the Pankhurst's announced that all decisions would be made by them alone. Mrs Pankhurst regarded the WSPU as an army, with her and Christabel as the generals and the membership the soldiers who would carry out orders. They would not countenance individuals committing acts of militancy of their own volition, such as Emily Wilding Davison when she took it upon herself to set fire to pillar boxes in London.

"Still, I'm not sure I would chain myself to railings outside the Houses of Parliament, or if I could even find the time to do so," said Letty, looking at Wilf for support.

"You must think about it and decide for yourself Letty dear," he said.

"Very well Rose," she said, turning back to Rose, "I promise I shall give your suggestion careful consideration."

"Thank you Dr Letty, that's very fair of you."

Wilf looked at the clock on the wall, which showed it was almost two o'clock, and said, "It's time to get back to work before there's a queue outside for the afternoon surgery."

They all got up and left the kitchen, Wilf and Letty to their consulting rooms and Rose to open up reception and the front door.

6

4 HATTON PLACE

THAT EVENING

I t had turned into a very cold evening and the fire burned brightly in the large, marble fireplace, casting shadows around the softly-lit room, the heavy, blue velvet curtains keeping out the night's chill draught.

Louisa was in the drawing room waiting for Charles to return. She was sitting by the cosy fire, sipping a dry sherry. She looked around the sumptuously decorated room with its deep pile Persian carpet in varying hues of blue. The sofas were upholstered in a contrasting gold brocade.

She sighed deeply, a frown on her usually smooth forehead. At fifty-one she was still a beautiful woman, with intelligent blue eyes which could express deep empathy for the women victims of serious crime who she worked with at the High Street police station. Her greying temples, which contrasted sharply with her auburn hair, was the only sign of her getting older.

"How did we manage to get it so wrong?" she thought to herself. Evangeline, who had been a very bright, sweet-natured, if determined, child was giving her parents great cause for concern and she had been doing so, progressively, since joining the suffragettes. "Damn them to the pit of hell!" she said to the empty room. She wasn't in the habit of using profanity and the fact that she did so now was testament to her agitation and concern for her daughter.

Until just over two years ago, their lives had run along smoothly and Evangeline had been half-way through her medical degree course at Edinburgh University, following in the footsteps of her father and Aunt Letty.

She came out of her reverie when she heard the sound of Charles's motor carriage crunching on the frosty gravel of the driveway. Charles had recently bought an Austin Landaulette and it was his pride and joy when he was home from Westminster. He loved getting behind the wheel with its dark blue and gold-trim paintwork. Louisa, who had also learned to drive, used it while Charles was in London. She would happily drive him to the Waverley Station to get the London train and she would collect him from there when he came home.

She went into the vestibule to meet him and helped him out of his woollen overcoat. He kissed her and said, "Thank you Louisa dear. Is our daughter home?" He wore a grave expression.

"No Charles," she said, hastily raising her hand to stop the tirade that was about to fall from his lips, "I telephoned her this afternoon at her office and she told me she was running late. Apparently her organiser, Jessie Gilhooley, was assaulted by her husband and Evangeline took her, firstly to the Royal Infirmary for an X-ray and then to her home to get some belongings as she was not returning home, at least for the time being."

She laid her hand on his arm and continued, "She's been a good samaritan today and has promised to be here by eight o'clock, or a little after. Come into the drawing room and I'll pour you a drink."

Resigned to the situation, he sighed and followed her into the warm, welcoming room.

She handed him a glass of brandy and sat down beside him. "Tell me about your day at the constituency office," she said, "while we wait for supper to be served."

It was eight-thirty by the time Evangeline arrived home and her parents were waiting in the drawing room with their after-dinner coffee.

Louisa got up and embraced her daughter, saying, "You must be frozen, would you like some coffee, the pot's fresh?"

"Yes, thank you Mother," she said, rather stiffly, Louisa thought, as Evangeline gave a side-long glance at her father.

She took the proffered cup and saucer and sat in a comfortable chair by the fire. Evangeline was the image of her mother at that age, with her thick auburn hair and clear blue eyes. She was a petite woman who took care with her appearance and she always wore fashionable clothes. After taking a sip of the coffee, she looked directly into her father's eyes and asked, "So what's the emergency Father? Why the summons?"

Charles looked at his daughter with a mixture of frustration and concern, although frustration was the stronger emotion. "I am going to ask you a direct question Evangeline," he said evenly, "and I would appreciate an honest answer."

She nodded and said, "Go on Father."

"Did you set fire to John Sinclair's house in Charlotte Square last night?"

"I heard there had been an attempted arson attack, but what makes you think I had anything to do with it?"

"Oh come Evangeline," he said, annoyed at her prevarication, "it doesn't take a great leap of imagination to put the facts together." He got up and began to pace the room. She really had a way of getting under his skin.

Her mother threw her a warning look but Evangeline refused to meet her gaze. She sat still and erect and said nothing.

"You didn't come home last night and you stayed the night at your grandparents house in Heriot Row which, incidentally, is not that far away from Bute House in Charlotte Square."

Evangeline looked at her father with disdain and replied, "I'm glad you took up medicine and not law Father, since that hardly constitutes evidence against me," she said, lifting her chin and looking down her nose at him, despite the fact that she was sitting and he was standing. "For your information," she continued imperiously, "not that I have to account to you for every minute of my day, I was at a meeting in Florence McVie's house in Melville Street and it ran on until almost midnight."

"WSPU literature was found at the scene," her father retorted.

"Again," she said, "that is circumstantial. Do you know how many WSPU members there are in Edinburgh? Any one of them might be responsible. I say "might be" since it could well be anti-suffrage people - probably men - who planted *evidence*," she emphasised the word, "to make us out to be criminals."

"I think that's a very flimsy argument Evangeline, given that it has become the calling card of the suffragettes at every public outrage committed in the past two years - from assaulting politicians to smashing windows and setting fire to letterboxes," Charles said angrily.

"Exactly, thank you for proving my point, and, by the way, the police came to the office today and they were satisfied with my whereabouts last night, even if you are not," she said, standing up. "Now, if you'll excuse me, I'm rather tired after a hard day and I'm going to bed. Goodnight Mother," she said to Louisa who had remained silent throughout the heated exchange between father and daughter.

He caught her arm as she tried to flounce past him. "Not so fast young lady, I have not finished."

She considered pulling away from him and continuing up to her room, but she thought better of it. She knew she had already crossed the line to being disrespectful with her remark about his choice of career. Instead, she stood opposite him, mutinous, with arms folded.

"Do you realise how much embarrassment you cause me, as a Liberal Member of Parliament, when my daughter, my only child, is part of a national campaign of social disobedience and active militancy against a government that I am part of?" Charles was president of the Board for Education.

"Well, do you know how much you embarrass me?" he asked again, when she did not answer.

"I can't help that Father," she replied coldly. "Perhaps if you had stood as a Labour candidate, there would be no need for embarrassment. We have supporters in the Labour Party."

"Labour would never get voted in here and well you know it." By this time, Charles was beginning to feel a deep tiredness creeping through his body. He sat down heavily and said, "Sit down Evangeline, please."

"I'd rather remain standing if you don't mind." She liked the fact that he had to look up at her.

Louisa spoke for the first time, "Evangeline dear, please do as your father asks and sit down." Seeing the pained look on her mother's face, she sat on the edge of the armchair she had just vacated.

Charles was silent for several moments, carefully weighing up his words. When he had, he said, "Evangeline, by being a member of the Women's Social and Political Union, you are willingly sanctioning militant and criminal acts. I don't know what your part in those crimes has been, apart from being arrested in Dundee last May." He paused and looked at her, trying to gauge her reaction to his words. Her poker face gave nothing away, so he went on, "I don't know if you were personally involved in last night's arson attack on the home of Sir John Sinclair, but I am having some difficulty believing your story. I am very uncomfortable with the thought that I might be harbouring a criminal under our roof and it doesn't sit well with me, both as a doctor and a member of parliament ,that you or what you stand for, are willing to put people's lives at risk."

"But the house was empty last night and no one got hurt," was her knee-jerk reaction. "I read about it in today's newspaper." she added quickly.

"Perhaps not this time Evangeline, but if it hadn't been for the quick reaction of that constable and the timely arrival of the fire brigade," he shook his head sadly, "the lives of the domestic staff and the people in the adjoining buildings could have been at risk if the fire had got out of control."

She sat, thoughtful, her expression still mutinous, then she said, "So, you are throwing me out of my home?"

"No!" exclaimed Louisa, "that's not what your father is saying."

"Well, let's put it this way darling," he looked at Louisa, "either Evangeline ceases her militant activities with the suffragettes or she must find herself somewhere else to live. Having her living here is tantamount to condoning the actions of that organisation. Don't you see that Louisa dear?"

"I do Charles," she replied sadly, then turning to her daughter she pleaded, "Evangeline my dear, why don't you give up the WSPU and come back to the NUWSS?"

Evangeline sighed sadly and, shaking her head, she replied, "You don't understand, do you Mother? For fifty years you, Aunt Letty and my grandmothers have worked hard, trying to get the franchise extended to women by constitutional means. Think about it: five long decades of petitions, marches and processions and you are no further forward - in terms of women getting the vote - than you were in 1867."

"We have many MP allies in parliament, including your father. We just need to keep going in a peaceful manner. We have to be patient Evangeline, although I know it is difficult, especially for you younger women."

Evangeline looked kindly at her mother and said, "It's not enough Mother, we could be in the same position in another fifty years time. We need to be heard rather than seen in some pathetic procession that has no teeth. Almost daily, we have publicity in the press, our cause is getting the publicity because of what the suffragettes are doing - *Deeds not words* - and that is what we are demanding from this Liberal Government, deeds, not just saying we will get the vote but actually *giving* it to us. Can't you see that Mother?"

She got up to leave the room and Louisa asked, "But where will you go Evangeline?"

"Don't worry about me Mother, I have my allowance from dear Grandpapa that he left me in his will. I'll find somewhere and, in the meantime, I'll stay in the flat above the office."

"Stay until the morning at least," Louisa pleaded, "you don't have to leave tonight, does she Charles?"

"Of course not. It's too late and too cold tonight. Get a good night's sleep Evangeline, perhaps after you've slept on it, you'll change your mind."

"I won't, change my mind that is, but thank you Father. Goodnight Father, goodnight Mother," she said kissing Louisa's cheek, then she left the room leaving her parents feeling battered and bruised.

7

A LITTLE LATER

C harles and Louisa sat in silence for a long time after Evangeline had gone upstairs. Maggie came in to clear away the coffee pot and cups and, unusually for Maggie who liked to hear snippets from her employers conversations, the atmosphere in the room was such that she quickly collected the dishes and left, saying only, "Goodnight Sir Charles and Lady Louisa."

This brought them back to the present moment as both had been deep in thought. Charles put his head in his hands and said, "Good God Louisa, what have I done? I sounded just like my father when he gave Letty the ultimatum to do as he wished or she wouldn't be welcome under his roof."

In 1897, Letty, Charles's sister and a doctor in the Salisbury Medical Practice, had been brutally assaulted by the husband of one of her patients. Her father immediately ordered her to give up practising medicine and find a 'more suitable profession for a lady'. Letty refused and he had told her that if she insisted on disobeying him, she would no longer be welcome under his roof. Letty left home the following day.

"Don't be ridiculous Charles," Louisa said, more sharply than she had intended. Then more gently she added, "It's a totally different situation altogether, Letty was the victim of a crime, not *committing* one", she emphasised the word, "and she was a woman of almost forty, not a girl of twenty-two." Louisa had always found Charles's late father to be a bully where his daughter was concerned.

"But I can't help thinking that I sounded just like him and that history is repeating itself," he groaned.

"Nonsense Charles," Louisa said kindly, "you are not trying to control your daughter in the way your father tried to do with Letty. Remember how you talked him around, telling him he should be proud of her achievements in the face of such adversity?"

"Yes, you're right and she did deserve for him to be proud of her and to approve of her choice of career," he replied, nodding at the memory of the night he'd had the "man to man" talk with his father.

"Evangeline's situation is quite different," said Louisa. "For a start, she is condoning and sanctioning, supposing for one moment that she is not taking part in, actions which break the law. It's far from Letty's struggle to become a doctor. Evangeline threw her chance away, a chance that had come so easily to her. You cannot be seen to condone criminal acts, either morally or professionally Charles, you know that. Much as it pains me to see her go, I believe it is for the best while she is so heavily involved in the Pankhursts' WSPU."

Charles sat in thought for a few moments, then he said, "You're absolutely right Louisa dear, as usual. This business with Evangeline is nothing like what happened between my father and Letty. But I suppose it had to come to a head at some point."

"I think it's been building up for some time Charles, ever since she was arrested for throwing eggs at Mr Churchill in Dundee," Louisa replied.

"Yes, I was regarded with approbation after that and I know that some of my parliamentary colleagues talk about me, probably in terms of "not controlling" my daughter. Immediately after that incident, I would walk into a common room and find the room falling silent as I entered."

Louisa laid her hand on Charles's, "Oh Charles!" she said, with an expression of sympathy, "Evangeline has put you in a very difficult position, it has been far harder on you than on me," she laughed mirthlessly. "I get it from both my parents and your mother, but then they know what Evangeline is like and know they have probably contributed somewhat to her wilfulness, as well as us. Only Letty seems to be able to see the situation from both perspectives, although she thoroughly disapproves of Mrs Pankhurst's militant tactics."

"Churchill, in particular, gives me a wide berth as though I personally threw the eggs at him. He's so priggish that the image of him having eggs thrown at him gives me a guilty satisfaction." He looked at Louisa and they both began to laugh, a release for the pressure of the last few hours.

"You know Charles," Louisa said when they had stopped laughing, "I really do think it's for the best that Evangeline lives away from us, then she doesn't have to be deceitful or furtive and you, if you wish to do so, can let it be known in Westminster that you do not have anything to do with your daughter or her suffragette activities."

"Yes, I think I will do that Louisa. Difficult though this evening's exchange was, I do have a feeling of profound relief. Having said that, I don't know if I'll be able to look

John Sinclair in the eye when I'm back in the Commons on Monday."

"Do you think Evangeline lied to us about not setting fire to his home, that she was at some meeting elsewhere?"

"Oh Louisa," he replied, with a deep sigh, "I really don't know what to think, other than that I don't know my own daughter anymore."

Louisa squeezed his hand in a gesture of support and solidarity and said, "Let's go to bed, it's been an exhausting day."

"Yes Louisa, I think that's the best thing I've heard all day."

They went upstairs, switching lights off on the way, hoping for a peaceful, dreamless sleep.

8 LAUDER ROAD

MID-NOVEMBER 1909

It transpired that Evangeline moved into her Aunt Letty's suite of rooms in her paternal Grandmother's house in Lauder Road. It hadn't taken her long to persuade her grandmother to let her move in and, if truth be told, her grandmother had been very lonely, since being widowed two years previously, in the large house on her own with just a live-in housekeeper and her elderly lurcher, Rosie, for company.

Sitting in the drawing room, having coffee after supper, on one of the rare evenings that Evengeline was at home, Charlotte Frobisher said to her granddaughter, "Evangeline my dear, don't you think you're going to alienate the government with all this smashing of windows and setting fire to people's property?"

Evangeline rubbed the ears of Rosie, who was cuddled up next to her on the sofa, and replied, "We don't think so Grammie, and Mrs Pankhurst has sanctioned our actions provided nobody is hurt, it is only property after all."

"Nobody has been hurt, *so far*," Charlotte emphasised the words, "but accidents can happen Evangeline and even when you don't intend to hurt anyone, someone, or several people, may get hurt, or worse still, killed at some point in the future."

She strongly suspected that her beautiful granddaughter and only grandchild, since Letty had not produced any children, had been involved in the arson attack on the Scottish Secretary's home in Charlotte Square earlier that month.

"Don't worry Grammie," she said reassuringly, as she gently stroked Rosie's long-haired coat, "we plan everything carefully and to the last detail. We do our homework and gather intelligence on our targets."

"Oh Evangeline!" cried her grandmother fretfully, "please, don't tell me any more, I don't want to be an accessory to anything criminal."

"It's really alright Grammie, I've merely told you about our methods, that's all."

Mollified, Charlotte said, "Tell me about this Christmas Fayre you mentioned earlier."

"Oh we're so excited Grammie, it's going to be marvellous with lots of stalls and Mrs Pankhurst is coming to give a speech on the last day."

"Do you have a confirmed date and venue yet?" her grandmother asked.

"Yes, it's being held in the Waverley Market from Friday the 17th to Sunday the 19th of December," she gushed, "and WSPU members are coming from all over the country. Over a hundred stalls have already been booked to sell a variety of items from hats to home-baking."

"I remember the Faye we organised in the summer of '87 when we were raising funds so that two of your Aunt Letty's companions could take up their offer of places at the medical school in Dublin," she smiled at the memory. "You see those girls weren't as well off as Letty and the others. You were just a baby then and it was such fun and we had competitions too."

"Really Grammie? That's a good idea," said Evangeline, "what kind of competitions?"

"Oh, all kinds. Did you know that your mother took part in a whistling competition?"

Evangeline laughed, "Really? I never knew that," she said, impressed.

"And there was a clothes-washing contest for men, it was absolutely hilarious." Charlotte was enjoying her stroll down memory lane.

"We're going to have a replica of a prison cell with a wardress outside and people can go inside and see what it is really like for the price of 6d. But we're stopping short of the torturous force-feeding mock-up, that would be just too gris-ly." she shuddered at the thought of it and was glad it hadn't yet been used in Scotland.

"We're going to have commemorative programmes printed for sale too, it's all going to be wonderful fun and a great fundraiser. You will come, won't you Grammie?"

"I'm not sure if your father would approve Evangeline dear," Charlotte replied.

"Father doesn't need to know about it, does he?" asked Evangeline, with that stubborn jut of her chin which they had all come to know well ever since she'd been a young child. "Maybe Grandmama Moncrieff will go with you. It would be so good to have my grandmothers there, even if my own parents won't attend," she entreated.

"Alright then, I'll come, but only if Emily agrees to go too. I'll telephone her tomorrow," Charlotte agreed.

"I'd love to stay and chat longer Grammy, but I must go up to my study as I still have lots to do for this event," Evan-

geline said, getting up and kissing her grandmother on the
cheek.

ON THE LAST Saturday in November a double-page
advertisement for the Christmas Fayre appeared in the
Scotsman and the *Edinburgh Evening News* as follows:

"Grand W.S.P.U. Christmas Fayre!
Friday 17th - Sunday 19th December
in the Waverley Market
All kinds of stalls, competitions, music & demonstrations
Fun for all the family
GUEST SPEAKER:
Mrs Emmeline Pankhurst
will address the audience and close the Fayre
on Sunday 19th
TICKETS 2/6d
COMMEMORATIVE PROGRAMME 5/-

THE ADVERTISEMENT APPEARED with holly and decorations
around it and posters announcing the event were printed in
the WSPU's adopted green, white and purple colours.

CHARLOTTE HARDLY SAW Evangeline in the days leading up
to the opening of the Fayre as she left the house early in the
morning to go to the office in Drummond Street and she
didn't return until at least ten o'clock at night. She was,
however, glad to see a tailing off of the militant activities in

December, at least in Edinburgh, and she was glad and relieved that Evangeline was too busy with organising the Fayre to be taking part in any window-smashing or fire-setting.

She dined with Louisa every Wednesday evening when Charles was in London and they both came to Lauder Road for supper on alternate Saturdays. She was sometimes invited to the Moncrieffs for a dinner party, but she always felt out of place being the only woman there without a man accompanying her.

Her thoughts moved to her late husband, as they so often did. What a pity Henry died so suddenly two years ago, she thought, Letty was always worried about his heart with his volatile personality. She hadn't thought that losing her stubborn and difficult husband would leave such a void in her life. She had vowed, at the time, not to be a burden on her family and she congratulated herself on succeeding. Still, she often felt lonely.

Her thoughts turned to Letty and Wilf, who were extremely busy doctors, especially Letty, as she also ran the birth control clinic in the High Street. They came to dinner once a fortnight when they were not on call. She had hoped that Letty had married in time, at the age of thirty-nine, to produce some grandchildren for her, but it was not to be, apparently, and it would certainly not happen now at the age of fifty-one.

Charlotte gave herself a mental shake and decided not to let her thoughts take her to the negative "what ifs". She reminded herself of all the good things she still had in life as she stroked the head of her faithful hound who was lying sleeping on the sofa beside her.

"Come on Rosie old girl, it's time for bed and time for your last ablutions." Rosie, who knew the routine well, got up and stretched her long fawn-coloured body; front legs straight out in front of her with nose between her paws and bottom in the air, then she reversed the position, gave herself a good shake and wagged her tail, letting her mistress know that she was now ready to move.

9

SALISBURY ROAD

DECEMBER 1909

I t was a great source of sadness for Letty and Wilf that they had not been blessed with children and it wasn't for the lack of trying. They both enjoyed a deeply satisfying physical relationship and Wilf often marvelled at his good fortune in having such a responsive wife, despite the fact that it had not resulted in any babies. Instead, over the past ten years or so, they had directed their parental affection to Maisie's children.

Maisie Gallagher had been a patient of Letty's and it was Maisie's husband who had brutally assaulted Letty in her consulting room over a decade before. It was only due to the quick actions of Wilf that Letty had escaped being raped by Thomas Gallagher. He was subsequently tried and sentenced to life imprisonment which left Maisie and her five children without any means of support.

After a short period staying with her husband's sister, who was as horrible as he had been, Maisie found herself homeless and had no option but to enter the Edinburgh Poorhouse.

That was the worst day of their lives since they hadn't

known that the whole family would be separated with the two youngest, baby Ellen and Billy, who was only two and a half years old, going to the nursery. Thomas and John went to the men's wing and Maisie was left with just Mary, the oldest at eleven years. Throughout the following five miserable months Maisie cursed Tam Gallagher to the pit of hell.

Not long before Christmas 1897, almost six months after entering the Poorhouse, Maisie and her children were rescued by Letty and Wilf, except for Thomas, who had been boarded out, without Maisie's knowledge, not long after the family had gone to the Poorhouse. The Governor would not disclose Thomas's whereabouts until Wilf persuaded him, under threat of losing his tenure there. Wilf had brought Thomas home to his mother in a very poor and emaciated state.

Maisie and her family were housed in the Mews flat in return for Maisie's domestic services in the medical practice and the rooms above where Letty and Wilf lived.

There had been fears that Thomas might have contracted Tuberculosis during his boarded out period, but with Wilf's careful monitoring and Maisie's feeding, he made a fair recovery, although he was left with delicate lungs.

Mary, now twenty-three years old, had been encouraged by Letty to read books and work hard at school and was now working as a primary school teacher at the nearby St Leonard's school. She had been in total awe of Letty, whom she regarded as the saviour who rescued the family from the misery of the Poorhouse and she had, unconsciously, adopted Letty as a role model. She had become a member of the NUWSS as soon as she turned sixteen and she was very active in the organisation. The rest of Maisie's children, apart from twelve year old Ellen, who was about to go to secondary school, had done well and were either tradesmen or, in Billy's case, starting an apprenticeship with a local painter and decorator.

WHEN MAISIE CAME into work for her afternoon shift, she stopped to talk to Rose at reception. Looking worried, she said to Rose, "Mary tellt me that ye'd asked her if she wants tae join the Women's Freedom League wi' ye, is that right?"

Rose noticed the concern on Maisie's face and replied, "Aye Maisie, that's right, Ah feel we should be daein' mair than just signin' petitions an' gon oan marches."

"But thae suffragettes are breakin' the law wi' their smashin' windaes an' settin' fire tae pillar boxes. Ah'm no' wantin' Mary gettin' arrested an' maybe losin' her job at the school." Maisie wasn't able to keep up with the differences between the various women's suffrage organisations and what they stood for, and she wasn't alone in that since the newspapers, especially the tabloids, tended to tar them all with the same brush.

Rose tried to reassure Maisie, she said, "No Maisie, the members of the Women's Freedom League are against violence, they jist want to be a bit mair active, ye ken. In fact the WFL was founded by women who left Mrs Pankhurst's lot because they were opposed tae the violence an' the way Mrs Pankhurst and her daughter were runnin' the organisation - keepin' control an' no' lettin' anybody else make decisions. Excuse me a minute," she said, when a patient approached the reception window.

While Rose saw to the next three patients, Maisie went to her utility cupboard, took off her coat and hat and put on her wrap around apron. She gathered up her cleaning materials and when she went back into the corridor by reception, Rose said, "Maisie, Ah'll explain it a' tae ye when ye've finished, but honestly, there's no anything tae be worried aboot."

"A'right hen," replied the easy-going Maisie, "ye can explain it tae me then," and she went about her work of mopping and dusting the practice.

Rose, who was now thirty-six, had worked for Letty and Wilf for the last fourteen years and was a young widow. She had married a young police constable, Kevin Nicholson, in 1900 and six months after the wedding he was killed in the line of duty, whilst attempting to rescue a child from the second floor of a burning tenement building.

The child had been lowered to safety from the second floor window to the ground, whilst Kevin had braved the smoke and flames in the stairwell, as he struggled up the first flight of stairs. Tragically, he was overcome and his body was found later by firemen after the blaze had been extinguished.

Rose, who was never the same again, had spent all her free time submerging herself in her suffrage work and her part-time job at the family planning clinic. As an attractive woman, she had received numerous invitations from men to go to the theatre or for a meal, but she politely turned down all invitations, determined to live her days out as a widow.

10

19TH JANUARY 1910

E dinburgh in December 1909 had been relatively peaceful, in terms of militant activities, since the suffragettes had been busy organising the Grand Christmas Fayre which had been a spectacular success as record funds had been raised and many new members had joined the WSPU.

The audience of thousands in the Waverley Market were spellbound by Mrs Pankhurst's inspiring speech and her words still rang in the mind of Evangeline Frobisher who travelled in the first class carriage of the Edinburgh to Dundee train. Her mother was right when she had said she was in thrall to Mrs Pankhurst and she relived the closing speech given by her mentor.

"We shall be marching to Parliament, not as law break-ers, but because women should be law makers. A society that allows women no part in decision-making, cannot flourish. Beyond the home, what lives are we permitted? Important posts are barred to us in all professions. Posts in government are just for men. Yet all their decisions affect women.

They must either do us justice, by giving us the vote, or do us violence! Votes for women."

A loud and lingering cheer had gone up at the end of the speech.

The Prime Minister, Mr Asquith had called a general election in January 1910 and this provided the suffragettes with a great deal of scope for their militant activities throughout the United Kingdom, as members of parliament and ministers returned to their constituencies to run their campaigns for re-election.

JESSIE GILHOOLEY WAS to remain in Edinburgh and organise and co-ordinate her team of women who would target the three Liberal Edinburgh Members of Parliament.

In retaliation for the continual failure of Asquith's government to extend the vote to women, Mrs Pankhurst had instructed the WSPU to target Liberal candidates up and down the country. Edinburgh Central, South and East were held by the Liberals and a campaign of heckling and window-breaking had been planned for all three.

Meg McIntyre and Jean Kennedy, who had joined the Edinburgh Women's Suffrage Society with Jessie in 1897, had been persuaded by her to join the WSPU and they were all going to target the candidate for Edinburgh South, Sir Charles Frobisher.

Evangeline had been dispatched to Dundee to help the WSPU branch there, and cause as much disruption as possible to Winston Churchill's campaign. Even the rebel-lious and stubborn Evangeline thought that family relations were strained enough without her targeting her father or his Liberal colleagues in Edinburgh and she had decided to leave that in the very capable hands of Jessie Gilhooley.

Earlier the previous year, Evangeline had instructed members of the Edinburgh branch to join the Women's Liberal Federation, in order to gain entry to meetings and speeches held by Liberal politicians.

On the evening of Wednesday the nineteenth of January, Sir Charles Frobisher was due to give a speech at a rally in the Queen's Hall in Edinburgh's South Side and, beforehand, Jessie and her team of three, had their final briefing regarding their mission for that night.

"We will sit in silence until Sir Charles has been speaking for exactly thirty minutes," she said and, looking at her pocket watch, asked, "are we all on the exact same time? I make it seven-thirty."

"Yes," agreed the other two, checking their watches and adjusting them as necessary.

"Fine," said Jessie, "put on your hats and coats, it should only take us ten minutes to walk there and we want to be early enough to choose our seats carefully. Now, have you everything you'll need?" She looked at Meg and Jean who each had a particular task to carry out.

"Aye," they replied, secreting their implements inside their long winter coats.

By eight-thirty Charles was well into his speech, saying, "The Liberal Party has, since 1906, continued to fulfil its commitment to those in poverty, those who are injured at work and those who cannot otherwise support themselves, by implementing social legislation"

Cries of "Hear! Hear!" and cheering from the audience.

He continued, "In 1906 we passed the Workmen's Compensation Act. Also, that year, we passed the Education

Act to enable schools to provide meals for the children. The 1907 Education (Provisions) Act created medical inspections and in 1908 we passed the Coal Mines Regulation Act, limiting the working hours of miners to eight hours a day." More cheering.

"I now make this promise to you, if I am re-elected as Member of Parliament for Edinburgh South, I will do my utmost to ensure that we have a National Insurance Act in the near future which will help those on low wages or who are unable to work because of injury, old age, sickness or due to cyclical employment ... "

Just at that moment three things happened consecutively. Firstly, Jessie Gilhooley stood up and shouted, "When will the Liberal Government give women the vote?" To which several people, all men, replied with "Keep quiet or get out!"

Next, Jean Kennedy unfurled the WSPU banner and she shouted repeatedly, "Votes for women! Votes for women!" During this distraction, Meg McIntyre walked, unobserved, up a side aisle and she threw half a dozen eggs onto the platform where Charles stood. As she threw them, one by one, she shouted - one syllable per egg thrown - "That's for Mr Asquith!"

Five of the eggs narrowly missed Charles, but one found its mark and shattered on the front of Charles's jacket. He took his handkerchief from his pocket and wiped the mess as best he could.

By this time, two men, sitting where Meg was standing, got up and took hold of her by the arms and manhandled her down the aisle and out into the entrance foyer, where Jessie and Jean had already been dragged by other men in the hall, and were held in a vice-like grip

"Let me go, ye brute," cried Jessie, "ye're hurtin' ma airm!"

Meg and Jean were also struggling to free themselves from their heavy-handed captors and both were shouting at the tops of their voices," "Votes for women!" and "Deeds not words!"

"Shut up!" called the man holding Jean, "you're going nowhere until the constables arrive." Someone had been sent to fetch the police as soon as the heckling began.

Jean, Meg and now Jessie were all shouting, "Votes for women!" and "Deeds not words!" when suddenly Jessie felt a big hand trying to cover her mouth and she sunk her teeth into it, biting as hard as she could. The man released his grip on her arm and slapped her hard across the face and she let go of his hand, stunned. He had no hold on her now as he was nursing his injured hand, so she took advantage of her freedom and kicked him as hard as she could on his shin bone.

People from inside the hall came and gathered at the door, watching the melee when two police constables arrived, whistles blasting in a request for reinforcements.

The three women were ignominiously bundled into a Black Maria (police van) and taken to the Pleasance police station, while the reinforcements, who arrived shortly afterwards, took statements from the shocked witnesses, including Sir Charles Frobisher.

THE DESK SERGEANT took charge of them on arrival and booked them in, asking them to empty their pockets. Their banners had been seized at the Queen's Hall and Jessie, Jean and Meg, in turn, removed keys, handkerchiefs and money from their coat pockets, leaving the stones they always carried in case the opportunity for breaking windows arose. Thankfully for them, male police were not allowed to do a body search on women.

Later that night, Jessie tapped on the cell wall with a stone and, on receiving an answering tap from Jean and Meg, she tapped her stone repeatedly, shouting, "Votes for women! Votes for women!" Jean and Meg joined in until the tumultuous noise brought the duty constable down to the cells.

On hearing his key turn in the lock of the cell door, Jessie began throwing the stones at the high window of her cell, successfully breaking a pane of glass. She was sitting on the bed, looking defiant, when the constable entered. He took one look at the window and shook his head.

"Well lassie," he said, "it's you that'll be cold the night, no' me." That's a chilly east wind blowing through that hole in the windae and that'll be added to your list of charges. You'll be up before the sheriff first thing in the morning. Goodnight," he said and left the cell. The click of the key in the lock echoed through the silence.

11

EDINBURGH SHERIFF COURT

THURSDAY 20TH JANUARY 1910

T he three women stood together in the dock of the court, looking slightly dishevelled after a night in the cold police cells. The public gallery was packed with WSPU members and supporters and the section for newspaper reporters was full to capacity.

After swearing them in, the Clerk of the Court read from a sheet of paper. "Jessie Gilhooley, Jean Kennedy and Meg McIntyre, you are charged with a breach of the peace at the Queen's Hall last night - the 19th of January - during a political meeting where Sir Charles Frobisher was giving a speech."

He took another piece of paper and continued, "Meg McIntyre you are also charged with assaulting Sir Charles Frobisher with an egg."

There was laughter in the public gallery and someone shouted, "Well done Meg, ye gave him laldy!"

"Silence!" called Sheriff Robertson who was presiding over the case. "Continue Mr Grainger," he said to the Clerk of the Court, who proceeded to read the charge again.

"Meg McIntyre, you are also charged with assault by

throwing eggs at Sir Charles Frobisher, one of which hit him
on the chest. Jessie Gilhooley, you are also charged with
breaking the window of your police cell last night. How do
you plead?"

"Guilty," all three replied. The WSPU policy, at this
point in, time was to draw attention to the cause by being
arrested, going to prison and going on hunger strike. This
policy resulted in a great deal of publicity in the
newspapers.

"Very well," said the sheriff, "I must say that in my opinion, you would be well advised to get rid of the delusion of
the attainment of any political object by rowdyism of this
description. I am, therefore, imposing a fine of £5 or ten
days imprisonment on each of you."

There were calls from the women in the gallery which
varied from, "Shame!" to "Votes for Women!" to "They're
innocent, Asquith is guilty of breaking promises!"

"Silence!" called the sheriff for the second time, "or you
will be charged with contempt of court."

All three opted for imprisonment and had already gone
on hunger strike, having refused breakfast in the Pleasance
police station.

IN THE CALTON Gaol they were issued with shapeless prison
clothes with arrows pointing upwards. They were then
taken by a grim-looking wardress to three identical cells
which measured a mere nine feet by four feet. A wooden
plank served as a bed with a thin mattress and blanket over
it and there was a very small window high up on the damp
wall. It was very grim indeed, but they were consoled by the

knowledge that their deeds had bought the cause much publicity.

The Calton Gaol was notorious in Scotland for its harsh regime and bad food but after their first day on hunger strike, the governor ordered appetising meals for the hunger-striking suffragettes since even he realised that it wouldn't be difficult to refuse the disgusting offerings that the inmates were usually given.

Prisoners were allowed only one hour's exercise every day and the women used this opportunity to bolster one another and to strengthen their resolve to refuse food.

It was the third day of their ten day sentence and they were slowly walking around the yard when Meg, who was the slightest of the three, stumbled and almost fell but was caught just in time by Jessie and Jean.

"Are ye a'right hen?" asked Jessie, her face full of concern for her friend.

"Aye, Ah'm jist a wee bit light-heided fae the lack o' food, but Ah dinnae ken if Ah'll manage any exercise the morn, Ah feel that weak."

"Ah ken it's no' easy Meg," said Jean, "but we're luckier than the women in Holloway and other English prisons where they've been force-feeding these past couple o' years." She shuddered as she thought of the brutality of it.

"Ah think it's only a matter o' time before they start daein' that here, but we mustnae gie' in. No surrender!" replied Jessie.

"No surrender!" echoed the other two, feeling cheered by Jessie's words.

The women were further cheered by the fact that several WSPU members gathered outside the prison every morning at the exercise period and they kept up a chorus of chanting

"Votes for women!" "No surrender!" and sometimes they sang the women's marching songs.

By the next morning, all three were so weak that the prison medical officer, Dr Simpson, feared for the women's health if they continued to refuse food. By mid-afternoon, after receiving a telegram from the Secretary for Scotland, Jessie, Jean and Meg were released early due to ill health.

The January sun shone weakly as they emerged from the jaw-like doors of the Calton Gaol. They were jubilant, despite their weakened state and were met by a contingent of Edinburgh suffragettes and they were taken for afternoon tea at Jenners, where they were brought up to date on the progress of Evangeline and the others in Dundee.

12

4 HATTON PLACE

THE DAY AFTER THE QUEEN'S HALL DISTURBANCE

C harles and Louisa had just finished breakfast and Charles was reading an account in the *Scotsman* of the incident in the Queen's Hall the previous evening.

Louisa looked at his grim expression and asked, "Is the incident in today's newspaper Charles?" She had been distressed when Charles had come home with egg stains on his jacket and he'd told her about what had happened and the subsequent arrests.

"Yes," he said, "I'll read it to you."

He unfolded the paper and began, "Last night the police were called out to an incident in the Queen's Hall where Sir Charles Frobisher, sitting Member of Parliament for Edinburgh South, was giving a speech to Liberal Party members. Three suffragettes were arrested and charged with disorderly conduct and a breach of the peace.

Jessie Gilhooley and two others, named as Jean Kennedy and Meg McIntyre, entered the Queen's Hall under false pretences with the deliberate aim of disrupting the meeting.

About half an hour into Sir Charle's speech, Gilhooley stood up and shouted, "When will the Liberal Government give women the vote?" This was immediately followed by Kennedy unfurling a Women's Social and Political Union banner and repeatedly shouting, "Votes for women!" at the top of her voice.

Such was the distraction, that McIntyre made her way up a side aisle, unnoticed, and commenced to throw half a dozen eggs at the platform where Sir Charles was standing patiently, waiting for order to be restored.

The women were grabbed by several men in the auditorium and roughly manhandled out of the room. The constables were summoned and the culprits were driven off in a Black Maria to the Pleasance police station.

It was further reported by the police that, whilst in custody, the women caused another breach of the peace by banging stones on the walls of their cells and shouting "votes for women". It is understood that the prisoners failed to completely empty their pockets, thus retaining the stones for further disturbance. It is also reported that Gilhooley broke the window in her cell as a final act of defiance.

All three will be up before the bench at the Sheriff Court later today. We will bring you more on this story as it comes in."

Charles sat staring, as if in disbelief, at the article he had just read out to Louisa. It somehow seemed worse reading it aloud than when he had first read it moments earlier. He shook his head sadly and said, "I wonder where Evangeline fits into all this?"

"I spoke to your mother earlier Charles and she told me that Evangeline is on her way to Dundee on WSPU business."

"Oh no!" he groaned, "that can mean only one thing."

"What's that?" asked Louisa.

"Winston Churchill is in Dundee to defend his seat and I dread to think of what Evangeline and her friends will be getting up to."

Louisa blanched and said, "Oh Charles, I really do fear for our daughter. She's like a runaway train, there's no stopping her and she won't listen to reason."

"It may be worse than disrupting Churchill, you know, since Asquith will be in his East Fife constituency and that's not that far from Dundee," he said. "I suspect they'll import militants from down south to target those prime targets."

"I suppose if I were in their shoes it would make tactical sense," Louisa replied.

"Oh Louisa!" exclaimed Charles, "not you too! They talk of themselves as though they were an army, with those blasted Pankhursts as the generals waging a campaign of war on the British Government."

Louisa felt wounded by the way he had spoken to her and she said, "Charles, that's not fair and it's not like you. I was merely making an observation on the geographical proximity of both constituencies."

Immediately remorseful for his outburst, he went around the table and knelt beside Louisa, taking her hand in his. "I am so sorry my darling Louisa," he said, bowing his head and kissing her hand, "please forgive me. It must be the strain of such a difficult time and the estrangement from Evangeline, not to mention what happened last night, that has me so unbalanced."

"It's alright Charles, I forgive you," replied Louisa tenderly, "I know how much stress you're under. We both are, and have been for a while now, and not knowing what

Evangeline is going to get up to in Dundee just makes it that much harder to function normally."

"Louisa," said Charles, soberly, "I think we both have a good idea of what our daughter is up to in the North and I have a sneaking feeling that we will know for certain over the next few days as the Press are sure to be where the militant suffragettes congregate."

" Sadly, I think that's very true," Louisa agreed. "Oh Charles, do you remember the times when Evangeline made us proud, it seemed that our darling girl led a charmed life and we thought she would always be a credit to us?"

"I do," he replied, smiling. "I don't think I could have been prouder than when she passed the matriculation examination for the Edinburgh Medical School and she did so well for the first two years." His smile faded when he thought about her dropping out and giving up what could have been a promising career as a doctor.

"Perhaps this is just a phase Charles. She might get it out of her system and go back to medical school and complete her training and degree," Louisa said, feeling less hopeful than the words she spoke.

"Who knows what the future holds Louisa dear?" he said standing up again "Until then we must hope and carry on with our lives with our heads held high." He glanced across at the newspaper lying on the table and did not give voice to the feeling of dread sitting deep in the pit of his stomach. Instead, in a much brighter, if unconvincing manner, he said, "I must get along to my constituency office now my dear, I have several meetings scheduled this morning."

"And I must get ready for work too Charles. I have three

new clients today and I must try to rid myself of those thoughts of Evangeline and have a clear head for them."

Charles kissed his wife and said, "Have a good day Louisa, I shall be home around six o'clock."

"You too Charles," she replied, as he left the room.

13

DUNDEE WSPU BRANCH OFFICE

THURSDAY 20TH JANUARY 1910

While the Edinburgh Liberal MPs were being *visited* by the suffragettes there, Evangeline had been invited by Dundee activist, Ethel Moorhead, to stay with her for the duration of what they called the 'Churchill Campaign'.

Winston Churchill was due to give a speech on Friday the twenty-first of January at the Kinnaird Hall. A number of the Dundee branch members had gathered in their office in the Nethergate to plan their course of action for the disruption to his arrival at the hall and during the course of his speech inside the hall.

Ethel, who was one of the movement's most militant members, chaired the meeting of ten women, including Evangeline.

"You all know Evangeline Frobisher from Mr Churchill's by-election campaign in 1908," Ethel said.

"Oh we'd never forget Evangeline and her expert egg-throwing. Bull's eye, what!" said Maude, in her noticably upper-class accent.

"Churchill will arrive at the hall as close to two o'clock as possible so as to avoid any disagreeable confrontations with us, but we shall be ready for him," Ethel opened with the business of the meeting.

"Alright then," she said, "we shall need one group to meet Mr Churchill's car when he arrives, make sure you have a sufficient supply of eggs or rotten fruit - no stones - just softish food. We are just giving him a 'shot across the bows', so to speak. Who wants to do that?"

A petite fair-haired woman, who looked no older than a schoolgirl but who was, in fact, in her late forties, said, with an impish grin, "Winnie, Bridget and I will be the welcoming committee".

"Fine," said Ethel, "I'll leave that in your capable hands Dolly." She looked back at her list and said, "Who is going to volunteer to be the *Pied Piper?*" By this she was referring to someone to lead a large crowd through the streets to try to force the barricades that they knew the police would have in place due to previous disruptive behaviour when Churchill was in town.

"I'll do it," said Catherine Agnew, "I rather like the idea of being the Pied Piper."

"The rest of the Dundee members will be ready waiting for you at the top of Reform Street," said Ethel."Take Maude and Elizabeth with you and bring a fine crowd to applaud Mr Churchill's speech."

Looking at the remaining women, still to be given tasks, she said, "That leaves Evangeline, Peggy, Mary and me." She paused for a few moments, thinking, then said, "Mary, are you prepared to hide in the hall overnight?" she asked of Mary Maloney.

"I'll do whatever it takes Ethel," she said, agreeably, then asked, "Bell?"

"Of course," replied Ethel. Mary's 'party piece' was to

follow Liberal politicians around and ring a very loud, brass hand-bell whenever they attempted to speak.

"So," concluded Ethel, "Evangeline, Peggy and I will hide in the attic flat of the adjacent building in the Overgate, which, thankfully is rented by one of our members, a very strategic place to live, for our purposes anyway," she nodded, smiling. "From that vantage point we will throw missiles at the glass roof and the windows of Kinnaird Hall while Mr Churchill is speaking. Between that and Mary's bell, I think we can keep his speech curtailed for some time." They all agreed, laughing at the thought of the politician becoming extremely heated at the disruption, possibly even apoplectic.

"Excellent, see you in the police station tomorrow night, no doubt," Ethel said, bringing the meeting to a close.

Friday, 21st January

THE AREA around the entrance to the Kinnaird Hall was cordoned off by barricades and a large number of constables, as a crowd gathered waiting to cheer or jeer Mr Churchill's arrival. Suffragettes and their male supporters had been standing with their banners in a peaceful manner, as though lulling the constables into a false sense of security by their unusual calm and serene behaviour.

Members of the Liberal Party and the general public had been filing into the hall for the past half hour and it was now ten minutes to two. At exactly five minutes to the hour, a black Daimler turned the corner of the street and stopped in front of the Kinnaird Hall, as cheers went up from Mr

Churchill's supporters who had been awaiting his arrival with anticipation.

The chauffeur got out of the car and opened the door. On hearing the cheering, Mr Churchill paused momentarily to wave to them and it was at that moment that a tremendous noise broke out and shouts of "Votes for women!" erupted from the hundreds of suffragettes being held back by a deep cordon of police constables.

Churchill's expression of delight quickly changed to one of concern and even fear and, as he turned to hurriedly mount the steps to the hall, he was pelted with a barrage of eggs and rotten fruit. One particularly rotten apple was thrown with such force, it splattered on the back of his top hat, knocking it over his eyes, at the same time as an egg smashed on the back of his overcoat.

As they hurled the various pieces of fruit and eggs at the MP's body and motor car, Winnie, Bridget and Dolly shouted, "Votes for women!" "Voteless not voiceless!"

Once inside the hall, Churchill removed his overcoat and hat and inspected the damage. He handed them to an aide to be cleaned whilst he was giving his speech.

Meanwhile, outside the hall, Winnie, Bridget and Dolly were in a fierce altercation with the police who were trying to arrest them. Dolly, taking a whip from her capacious cross-body bag, rained a good blow to the side of the constable's neck before her arm was twisted painfully behind her back and the whip seized from her grasp. While one constable was holding her arm behind her back, another was trying to drag her towards the Black Maria which had drawn up at the hall just as Mr Churchill's car was driven away. The petite Dolly fought like a wild cat, spitting in his face and kicking him in the shins.

At the same time, as Churchill was being pelted with an assortment of missiles, Catherine, followed by Maude and Elizabeth, was marching down the street adjacent to the Kinnaird Hall, carrying a wide ribbon in the WSPU tricolours with words in big black letters, which read: "Follow me. Force the barricades, Votes for women!" She urged the crowds to follow her, her strident voice calling, "Follow me and force the barricades. Let us take our cause right into the hall and tell Mr Churchill that we want the vote."

By the time they reached the hall, hundreds of people rushed the police cordon and tried to gain entry. The number of local suffragettes had been swollen by many travelling from other parts of Scotland and further south.

Upon reaching the hall, Catherine, Maude and Elizabeth were grabbed by the police and bundled into the police van that held Winnie, Bridget and Dolly.

Slightly battered, but smiling widely, Dolly said, "Well I would certainly call that a triumph."

The constable in the van with them grunted and said, "We'll see how much of a triumph it is when you're up before the sheriff in the morning."

Meanwhile inside the Kinnaird Hall, the disruptive women having been dealt with and feeling confident that the unseemly incident had been quelled, Churchill, after being introduced, set about giving his speech.

Mary Maloney, who had been hiding in the cleaner's cupboard until the speech was under way, crept into a gallery above and to one side of the stage where Churchill was in full swing. She got into position and, at two-thirty exactly, she took the rag from around the bell's clapper and began to ring it, drowning out the politician.

Simultaneously, Evangeline, Ethel and Peggy leaned out of the window of the attic flat they'd concealed themselves in since early morning and began throwing stones at the windows and glass roof of the hall. Several missiles hit their targets and between the noise from the breaking glass and the clamour of Mary's bell, Mr Churchill's speech was effectively ended. He had no alternative but to give up and try another day. His car was sent for but the police advised him to remain in the hall until the women responsible for the disruption were apprehended.

It took some twenty minutes before Mary, still in the hall, and the others, trapped in the flat with no means of escape because of the number of constables in the street, were located and arrested for breach of the peace and disorderly conduct.

Mary was dragged, kicking and shouting, into the police van which had been sent for again after depositing the first lot of prisoners at the police station. She was locked inside while the constables continued to search for Evangeline, Ethel and Peggy.

The attic flat was discovered and the three women surrendered quickly to the police, at least until they were on the street and they discharged their remaining missiles over the heads of the police, breaking several more windows for good measure, all the while shouting "Votes for women!", "Voteless not voiceless!" and "No taxation without representation!" until the constables grabbed them by the arms and bundled them into the waiting van.

Their cries were taken up by the hundreds of supporters

who still thronged the street and their calls and shouts could still be heard as they were driven away to the police station to be charged on various counts of breaking the law.

14

DUNDEE SHERIFF COURT

22ND JANUARY 1910

A fter an uncomfortable but rowdy night in the police cells, the women were taken for trial before the Sheriff. The Dundee Courier reported the case as follows:

"LIVELY SCENES IN DUNDEE STREETS AND SHERIFF COURT

THE SUFFRAGETTES APPEARED in court in their three separate groups in order of their arrest as follows:

THE WELCOMING PARTY

This group consisting of Dorothea (Dolly) Smith, Bridget O'Dowd and Winifred (Winnie) Wallace who awaited the arrival of Mr Churchill's car and who proceeded to throw eggs and rotten fruit at him and his vehicle when he got out at the hall.

·   ·   ·

THE PIED PIPER PARTY

Catherine Agnew, along with Maude Greene and Elizabeth McPhie who gathered hundreds of followers and led them through the streets of Dundee to try to storm the police cordon around the hall entrance.

THE STONE-THROWING AND BELL-RINGING PARTY

Evangeline Frobisher, Ethel Moorhead and Mary Maloney who caused much noise and smashing of glass which effectively put a stop to Mr Churchill's speech and closed the meeting earlier than planned.

THE TRIAL GOT under way with the first group of three women in the dock. An extremely petite woman of around forty-five, called Dolly Smith, stood alongside Bridget O'Dowd and Winnie Wallace (all from Dundee). They all stood, looking defiantly at Sheriff MacKinnon as the Clerk of the Court read out the charges of: Breach of the Peace; disorderly conduct and assault on the person of Mr Winston Churchill, MP, with rotten fruit and eggs.

When asked "how did they plead?" Mrs Smith replied, "Does it matter? You'll find us guilty anyway."

The sheriff looked at her with a serious expression and said, "Mrs Smith, I advise you to answer "guilty" or "not guilty", otherwise you will be held in contempt of court and you will have that added to your other offences."

When she replied, "Oh go on then, guilty." there was much laughter and cheering from the public gallery which was filled to capacity with supporters of the nine women on trial.

Having had their fun, the other two replied with a proud

"guilty". Sheriff MacKinnon sentenced them each to a fine of two pounds or ten days in prison. They opted for prison.

Next in the dock were Catherine Agnew, Maude Greene and Elizabeth McPhie (all from Dundee or surrounding area) who were accused of disorderly conduct, and a breach of the peace by encouraging a crowd to rush the police cordon in order to gain entry to the Kinnaird Hall and disrupt Mr Churchill's meeting.

They all made guilty pleas and before sentencing them, the Sheriff singled out Catherine Agnew, as the "Pied Piper" and addressed her as follows:

"Although this charge is one of breach of the peace, it comes very near to something like incitement to riot. Had it not been for the admirable arrangements by the police, it might have culminated in something much worse. You are all three sentenced to a fine of forty shillings or ten days imprisonment."

Miss Agnew replied, "I speak for each of us here, each and every suffragette Sir, when I say that our actions are for political reasons in political agitation and we shall go on hunger strike whilst in prison."

Sheriff MacKinnon concluded by saying, "The consequences of your sentence is a case for the prison authorities. Case dismissed."

The women were escorted back down to the cells to a tumultuous applause from their supporters in the gallery, to await transportation to Dundee Prison when all the cases had been heard.

Next up was Mary Maloney (of Glasgow), Evangeline Frobisher (of Edinburgh) and Ethel Moorhead (Dundee) who were charged with breach of the peace, and disorderly conduct, with Misses Frobisher, and Moorehead also being charged with malicious damage to property.

When Miss Maloney was about to respond to the Clerk of the Court's question of a plea, a great clanging of bells erupted from the public gallery with such a deafening noise that the Sheriff's gavel could hardly be heard. Police were dispatched to eject the culprits and peace was eventually restored to the courtroom.

Once again the Clerk of the Court asked, "Miss Maloney, how do you plead?"

She smiled and looked up at the now silent public gallery and said, "I take it that's 'guilty'"

The Sheriff addressed her, "Miss Maloney, I sentence you to a fine of one pound or five days imprisonment."

"I'll take the five days," she paused before finishing, "on hunger strike."

"Dismissed!" was the curt response from the Sheriff and she was led down to the cells. He couldn't help feeling that these women were toying with him.

Evangeline Frobisher and Ethel Moorhead, both known for their more extreme forms of militancy, were the last two suffragettes to be tried.

"You are charged with a breach of the peace and malicious damage to property by throwing stones, breaking windows and the glass roof of the Kinnaird Hall. How do you plead?" asked the Clerk.

Miss Moorhead spoke and said, "I shall save the court's time and plead guilty on behalf of us both. However, I wish it to be known to this court - and the wider society - that we are engaged in a political campaign for women's right to vote and we have been forced to adopt unconstitutional methods of protest. Yes, we are legally responsible but the moral responsibility lies with the Liberal Government, particularly with the Prime Minister, Mr Asquith, for failing to fulfil his promises to extend the franchise to women." She looked across to us, the reporters in the press area, and added, "I hope you managed to get all of that down gentlemen."

There was a great cheer from the gallery with calls of "Hear! Hear!" and "Votes for women!" Sheriff MacKinnon banged his gavel three times and said, "Silence in court! This is my final warning. If there are any further interruptions, each and every one of you will be held in contempt of court. Is that clear?" He glared at the men and women in the gallery and then turned to Miss Frobisher and Miss Moorhead and said, ""Miss Moorhead, Miss Frobisher, I sentence you each to a fine of five pounds or fifteen days in prison, plus five pounds damages for the glass you broke."

"We'll take the fifteen days," announced Evangeline, "and may we thank the good people of Dundee for the very special way they stood up for the women, showing that they are entirely in sympathy with us and not the government of Mr Churchill."

It was obviously a well-rehearsed double act and most appreciated by their supporters who applauded loudly when the two women were taken down to the cells to join the others waiting to go to gaol.

If, as promised, the women do go on hunger strike, be assured that we, at the Dundee Courier, will keep you updated on the progress of events.

JOHN MACKIE, Court correspondent."

IN THE PRISON, all six women were ordered to strip, bathe and put on prison clothes and were then led, by a sour-faced wardress, to the cells they would occupy for the next ten to fifteen days.

15

4 HATTON PLACE

MONDAY, 23RD JANUARY 1910

C harles and Louisa were having a pre-supper drink when the telephone rang. A few moments later Maggie entered the room and said, "It's Mrs Frobisher Senior on the telephone for you Sir Charles."

A frown creased Charles's forehead. Something must be wrong since his mother never telephoned in the evening.

"Thank you Maggie," he said, putting his glass of whisky down and getting up from the armchair by the fireside.

Louisa could only hear Charles's part of the conversation, even so, from the tone of his voice, it sounded like unwelcome news. She too frowned and knew it had to be something to do with their daughter and her trip to Dundee. She heard Charles say, "Try not to worry Mother and thank you for letting me know," before returning to the drawing room.

"Evangeline?" she asked.

He sat down heavily before replying and drained the contents of his glass in one gulp. "Yes, I'm afraid so," he said, shaking his head, "she's serving a fifteen day prison sentence for smashing windows and the glass roof of the Kinnaird

Hall while Churchill was giving a speech, or at least, trying to. Apparently, the meeting was cancelled after only half an hour."

"But how did your mother know Charles?" Louisa asked, puzzled.

"Our thoughtful daughter had arranged for a friend to deliver a copy of the *Dundee Courier* to Mother and it had a full and graphic account of the activities and court case of those bloody suffragettes."

"I expect it will be mentioned in tomorrow's *Scotsman*," Louisa said.

"I expect so," agreed Charles, "but that's not all, she's gone on hunger strike as well."

"Oh Charles no!" exclaimed Louisa, "I know just how determined she is and she'll see it through to the end. Thank heavens they haven't introduced forcible feeding in the Scottish gaols.

"I don't want to worry you Louisa, but the matter has been discussed this past while," he told her. "There are those who think the Scottish Prison Service is being too lenient and that they should start force-feeding hunger-striking suffragettes, both as a deterrent and to bring them in line with the English prisons."

Louisa's hand flew to her throat and she asked, "Do you think it will be soon?"

"I know for a fact that, after the arson attack on Bute House, the Secretary for Scotland is leaning heavily in that direction. Most hunger-strikers are released before they have served their sentence, some even just halfway through due to fears for their health. But I can't help feeling that's a bit of an incentive to go on hunger strike."

"Charles, surely you're not in favour of forcible feeding? Even though I disagree with and disapprove of their militancy, I would not wish that on anyone. By all accounts it's barbaric. I disapprove of their methods, but they're very courageous. I heard that some women have been force-fed forty or more times during various periods of incarceration in Holloway Prison." She shuddered at the memory of reading one woman's account of being force-fed.

"Of course not, Louisa, but what do you do when a woman refuses to eat?"

"Exactly what has been happening in Scotland so far Charles," she said spiritedly, "after all, even if they are released after serving only three or four days, they'll probably be so unwell for several days afterwards that they will virtually be completing their sentences at home, probably in bed, so I'd hardly call that freedom, would you?"

"No Louisa," said Charles, sighing, "there is a lot of truth in what you say and I am definitely not an advocate of feeding women with rubber tubes forced down their throats or up their noses, with its concomitant risks. Quite frankly, I cannot understand how anyone calling themselves a doctor can be party to such a barbaric practice."

"What are we going to do about Evangeline? Can we pay her fine and have her released that way?" Louisa asked, a little hope showing in her eyes.

"No Louisa, I doubt very much whether Evangeline would want that," he replied. "She was in a position to pay her fine herself but she chose imprisonment so she could go on hunger strike for the cause."

"You're right Charles, I was grasping at straws. Relations between us are bad enough without doing that." Louisa conceded.

"She would just go out and get herself arrested again, straight away. There is also the matter of criminal damages that she will have to contribute to. I think Mother said five pounds."

"Five pounds?" gasped Louisa, "Oh Charles that is a lot of money."

Just at that moment Maggie knocked on the door and entered the room. "Supper is served Lady Frobisher," she said.

They went into the dining room, trying hard to keep their concerns for Evangeline at the back of their minds and not spoil their appetite for the meal that Maggie had so carefully prepared.

16

DUNDEE GAOL

26TH JANUARY 1910

Meanwhile, in Dundee Gaol, the prisoners were segregated and were forbidden to talk to each other in the exercise yard. It was their fourth day on hunger strike and the prison governor had sent a telegram, first thing, to the Secretary for Scotland requesting permission to have the women force-fed. After four days without food he was worried about the repercussions on their physical and mental health.

By noon he had received a telegram asking for the prison medical officer to examine the women to assess whether they were well enough to be forcibly fed.

After examining the women the medical officer advised that of the nine on hunger strike, Evangeline, Ethel and Maude were fit enough for force-feeding. The doctor, James Lochrin, reported back to the governor that he feared Dolly Smith, with such a petite frame would not survive force-feeding and he recommended her early release. As for the remaining five, it was his opinion that they were not fit enough to be force-fed but he would keep an eye on them for the next two days and decide then, regarding early release if they had not taken food voluntarily.

The governor furnished the Scottish Secretary with the medical officer's recommendations and awaited his response.

In Edinburgh, Sir John Sinclair considered the prison doctor's recommendations at length and pondered on the best course of action.

He personally disliked the idea of a woman being held down by several wardresses while a doctor pushed a rubber tube up her nose and down into her stomach, but on the other hand, if a woman was to die in prison whilst on hunger strike, it would look bad for the government and only fuel Mrs Pankhurst's cause. Finally, he made his decision. He could not afford for any suffragette to die whilst serving a sentence, especially with a General Election taking place over the next two weeks.

Thus, by nine o'clock on the evening of the twenty-sixth of January, the governor of Dundee Prison had received the necessary permission to release Dolly Smith and to arrange for Evangeline Frobisher, Ethel Moorhead and Maude Greene to be forcibly fed.

AT TEN O'CLOCK THE following morning, as Evangeline was lying on her plank bed weak from her fifth day without food, since they had all began their hunger strike whilst in police custody the previous Friday, she heard sounds that chilled her to the bone, sounds that she never thought she'd hear during her current sentence.

"Who are they coming for?" she asked herself, as the heavy footsteps hurried along the corridor outside her cell.

There was another sound too, a clattering, like a trolley bumping over the uneven stone flags of the corridor floor.

Suddenly the footsteps stopped outside her cell door and she sat up on the edge of the bed, frozen with fear. There was a dull click as the door was unlocked and two doctors and four wardresses entered the room.

In a grim tone, Dr Lochrin asked her, "Miss Frobisher, are you willing to take food voluntarily?"

"No," she said hoarsely, "no surrender!"

"Very well," he said and he motioned to the wardresses, "hold her down on the bed and let us get this business over with."

A mix of emotions surged through Evangeline's body - terror, anger, a terrible urge to flee and the rush of adrenalin gave her a strength she hadn't known she possessed. She dodged the hands of the wardresses who tried to grab her and, picking up the slop bucket, she threw it at one of them. The bucket caught the woman in the chest and the contents, which fortunately for the wardress, was only urine, spilled down her apron. She then tried to reach the trolley containing what she regarded as the "tools of torture" but was caught from behind by Dr Lochrin and lifted off her feet. "Let go of me, let go of me," she screamed, kicking her legs and catching one of the wardresses who called out in pain.

Still struggling, she felt herself being dragged backwards and pushed down onto the bed. She was still thrashing about with her arms and legs when Dr Lochrin pinned her down by the shoulders and shouted instructions to the wardresses. "You two, get hold of her feet!" and, to the other two, "You come here and hold her shoulders and arms, don't let her move!"

A sheet was put under her chin and Dr Lochrin took a

thick rubber tube which had a funnel at the other end and was being held high by the other doctor. Evangeline tried to resist, turning her head from one side to the other in a frantic attempt to avoid the tube, but she was tiring from the monumental struggle.

Suddenly Dr Lochrin held her small head rigidly still with one of his big hands and then pushed the rubber tube up Evangeline's left nostril. An excruciating pain burst through her head, making her ears ring and her eyes felt as though they were being pulled out of their sockets. This was followed by what felt like a ripping of her throat and a searing stab in her chest as the tube was pushed down and down, into her stomach.

Eventually, after what felt like an eternity to Evangeline, when the doctor was satisfied that the tube was in place, he motioned to the other doctor to pour the sloppy mixture of milk and raw eggs into the funnel. Evangeline had no struggle left in her small body by this time and as soon as the liquid hit her stomach she felt the urge to vomit.

The removal of the tube was almost as horrendous as its insertion and she felt the soft membrane in her nose was being cut by the thick rubber. Once it was out, she vomited and fought to catch heaving, painful breaths. She felt the doctor take her pulse and then the doctors and wardresses left her lying in a heap on her messy bed. Sobs wracked her already painful chest and her nose bled profusely. She thought she was going to die when she heard a tapping on her cell wall and the voice of Ethel Moorhead saying, "No surrender!"

Evangeline, whose throat burned painfully, could only whisper, "No surrender!"

She lay like that for some time then stiffened as she heard the sickening sound of footsteps and a trolley in the corridor again. "Surely they're not coming back again already?" her feverish mind thought, but it went past her door and stopped outside Ethel's cell. She covered her ears as she couldn't bear the sounds of her friend being force-fed.

After some time, sore and exhausted, she fell into a fitful sleep. She was awakened at some point in the afternoon as her cell door was being unlocked and this time the two doctors were accompanied by six wardresses.

17

DUNDEE GAOL

FRIDAY, 4TH FEBRUARY 1910

Monday the seventh of February was the day that Evangeline Frobisher and Ethel Moorhead were due to be released, but the date was brought forward due to their weakened condition after enduring forcible feeding twice a day for eight days.

The medical officer, the prison governor and the Scottish Secretary were sufficiently concerned about the state of their health, particularly that of Ethel Moorhead who had developed double pneumonia after the eighth day. Sir John Sinclair sent a telegram ordering their immediate release since he could not afford to have any prison fatalities so close to the election and, privately, he was convinced that he was sending Miss Moorhead home to die.

Thus, on the morning of Friday the fourth, a very weak Evangeline and a seriously ill Ethel Moorhead were released. Dr Grace Cadell, a friend of Ethel and a suffragette herself, was waiting with a cab to take Ethel and Evangeline home. When Grace saw how ill Ethel was she was very concerned for her friend, fearing for her life.

Back at the Moorhead residence in Perth Road, she

immediately got Ethel into bed and carried out a thorough examination on the extremely thin and ill woman. Evangeline had been helped to bed by Beatrice, the Moorhead's maid, and told Grace would be along to see her after she had seen to Ethel.

Listening to Ethel's lungs through her stethoscope, she was appalled and such were her fears for her friend that she thought the authorities had released her so she could die at home and not in prison.

For days Grace tended to Ethel, making sure she was well propped-up in a sitting position since allowing her to lie down with infection in her lungs would be fatal. She spoon-fed her beef tea at first and gradually she progressed to milky puddings before giving her light, appetising meals. Ethel was in and out of consciousness for the first few critical days and was only vaguely aware of Evangeline's brief visits.

On one such occasion, after Evangeline had asked if Ethel was going to die, Grace replied, "Not if I can help it. Do you know, that fool of a prison doctor must have got some of that slop into her lungs? That is why she is so poorly."

Evangeline was shocked at this information and felt herself incredibly fortunate that it hadn't happened to her. She felt her own health and a little strength begin to return after a few days, although she was still very weak. She was able to take short walks around the Moorhead's garden and she thought that she might be well enough to travel back to Edinburgh in another few days time, although she was still very worried about Ethel.

She had been told that her father had telephoned on her first night there, but she hadn't been well enough to take the call and that Dr Caddell had spoken to him. Apparently, his mother had received a call from Jessie Gilhooley, informing her that Evangeline had been released a few days early and that she was staying at the Moorhead residence to recover from her ordeal in prison, and his mother had immediately called Charles to let him know, hence the telephone call.

He was satisfied with Dr Cadell's report on her health, although dismayed to learn about the force-feeding, but he agreed to wait until Evangeline was well enough to call her parents herself. Once Evangeline was convinced that Ethel was going to recover, she made arrangements to return to Edinburgh

Monday, 14th February

Meanwhile, in Edinburgh, Louisa had been trying to persuade Charles to allow Evangeline to come home to Hatton Place.

"Why don't we invite her here Charles, we can both make sure she is alright. Perhaps her experiences in the gaol will have put her off the militant activities." She tried not to sound wheedling, but she was so anxious to have her daughter back at home where she could look after her, if needed.

"Alright Louisa, she can come home on one condition and that is that she stops all involvement with the WSPU and their militancy," he replied. "What time are you and Letty collecting her from the station?" Louisa had asked Letty to come with her to assess her daughter's state of health. Letty had agreed, but only if Evangeline gave her consent.

"Her train gets into the Waverley at 10.30 tomorrow morning," replied Louisa. "May I have the use of the car tomorrow Charles, or do you need it?"

"You take it Louisa, I'll be at the constituency office all day tomorrow since polling ends on Tuesday."

"Thank you Charles, I hadn't wanted to bring her home in a hackney cab."

LOUISA AND LETTY were waiting on Platform 1 where the Aberdeen to King's Cross train pulled in on time. Louisa looked on, horrified, as her pale-faced and very thin daughter stepped down from the train. Evangeline hurried forward into her mother's outstretched arms and hugged her warmly. Louisa was scared to hug her too tightly as she was so fragile-looking.

"Evangeline my darling," she said when she stepped back, holding her at arms length, "how are you feeling? You look so pale and thin."

"Hello Aunt Letty," Evangeline said, pulling away from her mother and avoiding her question and searching gaze, "it's so lovely of you to come and meet me."

"Let's take you home Evangeline," said Louisa, linking her arm.

"Not to Hatton Place Mother," she said quickly. "Home to Grammie's in Lauder Road. I telephoned her last evening and she's expecting us."

"Very well Evangeline," said Louisa, trying hard to hide her disappointment. She took this as a sign that she had no intention whatever of giving up her militant activities.

They were settled in her grandmother's drawing room, sipping coffee and trying to make polite conversation, but the subject on the minds of the three older women was like a presence in itself.

Eventually, Evangeline could stand it no longer and said, "Look, I know you're all bursting to know what it was like to be in prison," she failed to mention the words "hunger strike" and "force-feeding". "However, I am not prepared to share those experiences with non-militant suffragists, so can we talk about something normal, now that this is out of the way?"

"Evangeline," said Louisa, "I was wondering whether you would let Aunt Letty look you over, you know, to make sure you are well after your ... er, time in Dundee," she finished lamely.

Evangeline took a deep breath and made a concentrated effort not to get annoyed with her mother. "I'm well Mother, Dr Cadell gave me a final check up only yesterday," she replied. "Really, there is no need to worry or fuss over me, I'm fine."

Louisa was deeply hurt by her daughter's words, but she tried to hold back the tears that threatened to spill over.

It was Charlotte who steered the conversation away from dangerous waters by matter-of-factly asking, "So, what are your plans now Evangeline? What's next my dear?" She smiled and Evangeline's slightly ruffled feathers settled.

"Business as usual Grammie, there is still much to be done and the voting in the General Election ends tomorrow, so we shall be making our presence felt at the polling stations in all three Edinburgh Liberal constituencies." She looked at her mother and said kindly, "Don't worry Mother, I won't be anywhere near Edinburgh South, or the others, for that matter. I shall be working behind the scenes."

Louisa felt greatly relieved to hear this. At least if she was at the WSPU office she couldn't be arrested. There seemed little point in asking Evangeline to return home on the condition stipulated by her father, so Louisa said nothing about it. Instead, she said, "I must be going now Mother-in-law, thank you for the coffee and it's lovely to see you Evangeline dear." She looked at Letty and said, trying to keep her tone light, "I'll take you back to work Letty, I've kept you away long enough."

"Thank you Louisa, I'd appreciate that," Letty replied. If truth be known, she wasn't in a hurry to get back but she too felt uncomfortable in the company of Louisa and her estranged daughter. It seemed that nothing had been healed there, she reflected sadly. They got up to leave and Louisa and Letty kissed Evangeline on the cheek.

"Goodbye Mother," she said, "and please don't worry about me." she added kindly.

"Goodbye Evangeline, Goodbye Mother-in-law," she said as she left the room.

"I'll see you out," Charlotte said, closing the drawing room door behind her.

As she showed them out, she put her hand on Louisa's arm and said, "Don't distress yourself Louisa dear, she's young with a determined and independent mind. She'll come around in time and I'll keep an eye on her, at least when she's at home."

"Thank you," said Louisa, trying not to break down at the older woman's kind words.

Louisa was silent on the short drive from Lauder Road to Salisbury Place and Letty did not want to intrude into what was obviously a difficult and emotional day for her friend.

Louisa stopped the car outside the Salisbury Medical Practice and burst into tears. Sobs wracked her body as Letty held her in her arms.

"Let it all out Louisa dear," she said, stroking her hair. "I know it's hard to believe at the moment, but things will improve in time."

When Louisa's sobs had subsided, she replied, "You're right Letty, it is hard to believe at the moment and I had such hopes that she would want to come home. False hope, as it's turned out."

"The rift between Evangeline and Charles is too deep at the moment for her to even contemplate going home to Hatton Place, especially now with the General Election going on," Letty said, "but don't give up hope. I'll try to get her to talk to me, I may not have lost all of my influence over my goddaughter." She smiled at Louisa and was rewarded with one of Louisa's lovely smiles.

"How are you feeling now Louisa dear?" she asked.

"Much better for having a good cry and a good friend to listen to me. Thank you so much for coming with me today Letty, it means a lot."

"You're very welcome. Take care Louisa and please give my love to Charles.

Letty got out of the car and Louisa drove home feeling better than she had felt all day.

Postscript

Some two weeks later, a parcel arrived at the Edinburgh Branch office for Evangeline. When she opened it she found a purple velvet box and inside was a medal. The leaders of the Women's Social and Political Union had medals made for the suffragettes who endured force feeding in prison. A ribbon in their purple, green and white colours was on a silver bar and the medal itself was inscribed with the words, "For Valour". Evangeline was totally surprised and delighted with this acknowledgment from the organisation's leaders.

18

THURSDAY 17TH NOVEMBER 1910

Nine months later Evangeline Frobisher, Jessie Gilhooley and Meg McIntyre were in a first class compartment of the Edinburgh to London train. Jean Kennedy had been left in charge of the WSPU office in Drummond Street. They were on their way to join a deputation of women, organised by Mrs Pankhurst, who would march on Parliament the next day in protest at what they felt was a gross betrayal by the Prime Minister, Herbert Asquith.

They had the compartment to themselves and they were discussing the recent, unexpected, and extremely disappointing decision by the prime minister to veto the Conciliation Bill which, if passed, would extend the vote to women who met the 'property qualification,' that is, to women who owned property.

The Bill had been introduced into Parliament in May 1910 and would give the vote to around one million women. It was hoped, by the government, that if even a proportion of women were enfranchised, the suffragettes would cease their militant activities which had long been a thorn in the side of the Liberal Government.

Mrs Pankhurst had called off all acts of militancy and violence whilst the Bill made its slow progress through the various stages in Parliament.

Evangeline, was particularly incensed. "All these months of inactivity have been wasted, we could have been doing a great deal of damage to the government and a lot of good for the cause," she bemoaned. "I'll bet Asquith never had any intention of allowing it to pass. Damn him to the pit of hell, where I hope he rots!"

"Ah'm that mad tae," said Jessie, shaking her head, "Ah feel like we've been twiddlin' our thumbs a' this time, apart fae the odd march and petitions, when we could have got our teeth intae some real militancy."

Evangeline smiled affectionately at her. Ever since Jessie's husband had assaulted her, the two women had become very close friends and there were some in the Edinburgh branch who believed they were more than just friends. Lesbian relationships weren't unknown in the WSPU membership, as the activities carried out by the women required them to work very closely together and there was tacit acceptance of these relationships.

"How many o' us will be on the march?" asked Meg, speaking for the first time.

"Mrs Pankhurst thinks between three and four hundred, but it will be a peaceful and dignified show of our solidarity. Banners and heads will be held high," she replied, "as well as showing our disappointment and displeasure with the Liberal Government, of course," she added.

Their banners were furled and stowed on the overhead luggage rack, along with their overnight bags. They were staying for only two nights and would return to Edinburgh on Saturday. Evangeline had arranged for them all to stay in a London house with a woman called Amelia Wainwright, who was a friend of hers from her university days.

"What time are we to be at Caxton Hall the morn?" asked Meg, who liked to know the details of their itinerary.

"Ten-thirty," replied Jessie, "that should gie enough time for Mrs Pankhurst to talk to us and get us into formation lines ready for the march on Parliament."

"Let's hope the weather stays dry," commented Evangeline before they all fell silent with their own thoughts.

Neither Jessie nor Meg had been to London before and both were feeling a mixture of excitement and awe at the prospect of the bustling city and being in the company of the famous Mrs Pankhurst and her daughters.

As the train puffed further on its journey south, daylight began to fade and all they could see of the darkening countryside was the occasional farmstead with lights shining warmly behind curtained windows. Jessie and Meg began to drop off and had been sleeping for some time while Evangeline was busy with a notepad, planning a fresh campaign of militant activities for their return to Edinburgh. It would be back to work and business as usual after the long hiatus while the doomed Conciliation Bill had made its torturously slow journey through Parliament.

When the train slowed down on its arrival at King's Cross Station, Evangeline gently shook the other two women.

"Come on," she said, "get your things, we've arrived."

19

CAXTON HALL

FRIDAY 18TH NOVEMBER 1910

A round four hundred women were packed into Caxton Hall in London and emotions were running high. The atmosphere was electric and the noise in the room was deafening. Since 1907, the WSPU had met there when there was a new session of Parliament and the meeting was always followed by a march to Parliament where a petition, demanding the vote, would be presented.

Today, however, it was more important and auspicious than in previous years because of the deep sense of betrayal by the Prime Minister when he'd made the decision not to allow any more time for the Conciliation Bill to get through Parliament.

Leaflets were printed and widely distributed throughout the country. They read,

"VOTES FOR WOMEN
W.S.P.U. 4 Clement's Inn
A

DEPUTATION OF WOMEN
WILL GO TO
WESTMINSTER
soon after noon on
FRIDAY NOVEMBER 18
To protest against the action of the government
in vetoing the Conciliation Bill
TO LOVERS OF FAIR PLAY
WOMEN VERSUS THE GOVERNMENT!
Will you come and umpire?"

A silence fell when Mrs Pankhurst and her entourage climbed the steps to the stage. Dr Elizabeth Garret-Anderson and Flora "The General" Drummond were amongst them.

"Ladies," she called out in a clear voice, "as you know, our fears of the Conciliation Bill failing have materialised. Mr Asquith has refused the Bill any further parliamentary time and I rather think that he had no intention whatsoever of letting us have the vote, even in its reduced form of extending the franchise to women who own property." Calls of "Hear! Hear!" and "Shame on him!" rang out.

"We ceased our militant operations in good faith and it is obvious that we have been tricked. We must march on Parliament and present our petition and demand the vote. And we shall do so in a decorous and dignified manner. We will protest against this decision peacefully. There will be plenty of time afterwards for a continuous barrage of militant activity. As is usual on these occasions the police will be making arrests but I don't think they will have capacity in the cells for all of us today." There were more cries of "Hear! Hear!" and much cheering.

Evangeline, Jessie and Meg sat in the middle of the hall, enthralled by Mrs Pankhurst's words.

"Very well," she said, holding her hands up for silence. "Very well," she said again, and looked around at the other women on the stage, "my friends here and I will lead the march on Westminster. To Parliament Square!"

"To Parliament Square!" cried the hundreds of women in the hall, as one voice.

The ranks of women marching six abreast followed Mrs Pankhurst and special guests. A few yards ahead of them, two women held WSPU banners high and were the vanguard of the deputation.

Various banners fluttered in the breeze all along the length of the procession and the streets were lined with people watching the spectacle.

Jessie and Meg chatted excitedly on the ten minute walk and they managed to position themselves around the twentieth row in the long line of marchers.

As those towards the front of the deputation rounded the corner into Parliament Square, they stopped suddenly, frozen by what they saw. A huge crowd of policemen were assembled, the number was later known to be six thousand, waiting for the women to arrive and what ensued was nothing less than abject brutality.

Six thousand Metropolitan policemen against three to four hundred unarmed and defenceless women. But, instead of arresting the women, as usually happened, there were violent clashes.

The women turned to retreat, but the police closed around them and they were trapped and at the mercy, or otherwise, of the law enforcement officers.

Evangeline, Jessie and Meg got separated as the lines of police launched themselves at the women. Meg, the slightest of the three, was picked up bodily and thrown into a crowd of men, the policeman who threw her shouted, "Do what you want to her mate!"

Two men held her while a third sexually assaulted her, lifting her skirt and making lewd comments to his friends. Meg's face burned with anger and humiliation and the man molesting her shouted, "Fling this one back mate, there's nothing worth grabbing here. Let's wait until they throw us something with some flesh on her." They all laughed as they threw the petite Meg into the path of other policemen where she fell flat on her face.

She was roughly hauled upright by her left shoulder and her arm was twisted painfully up her back. The pain was excruciating and she thought her shoulder had been dislocated. She passed out with the pain of being held up like this and she lay prone on the ground, where the officer had dropped her, like a sack of potatoes.

Meanwhile, Evangeline was grabbed from behind, her breast was twisted painfully as the policeman spat obscenities into her ear. She tried to free herself but she was thrown to the ground where she lay stunned for some moments, then she was pulled up by the hair and pinned against a wall while the brute put his hand up her skirt and tried to rip off her undergarments. Terrified, she screamed and tried to kick the policeman, spitting at him and trying to bite him.

A gentleman in a silk top hat tried to rescue her but he was beaten off by two burly officers and she was dragged down a side street, to be raped she was in no doubt, when suddenly a crowd of men appeared and she thought she was going to faint, terrified that she was going to be assaulted by all of them.

To her great relief, they set upon the policeman who ran back up the street into the melee. Women were a much easier target than the gang of toughs he had just encountered. They had no time for the East End police force which made up many of the numbers there that day.

What happened to Meg and Evangeline were not isolated incidents. The women were being systematically beaten, had their arms twisted up their backs and were sexually assaulted, regardless of age.

Evangeline tried in vain to find Jessie and Meg and just as she turned to go back to Caxton Hall to see if they had gone back there, a fist caught her on the side of the face and she fell to the ground. After some moments, she got up and, walked around in a nightmarish daze. Her injured eye was now swollen and closed as she witnessed women being repeatedly thrown to the ground, hauled up, and then thrown down again.

One woman, later named as Ada Wright, was thrown backwards and forwards in a crowd which, it came to light later, had been incited to violence by Special Branch officers. She was thrown onto the ground one final time where she lay with police officers towering over her. Evangeline saw her afterwards, lying against the wall of the House of Lords, surrounded by several anxious-looking women.

Elsewhere, Jessie suffered a similar fate when she tried to rescue a disabled suffragette who was being tipped out of her wheelchair by a thickset policeman. Unlike Evangeline or Meg, since she had been assaulted by her husband the previous year, Jessie never went anywhere without a stout umbrella which gave her a feeling of security, should she ever need to defend herself again.

"Oy!" she shouted, approaching the policeman from behind, "leave her alone, ye big brute!" She raised her arm and rained several blows on his back with her umbrella, then knocking his helmet forward, delivered multiple whacks to the back of his bull-like head.

However, to the policeman, her actions had no more effect than an insect buzzing about his head and body. .

He turned and, for a moment looked Jessie up and down, then said menacingly, in a Cockney accent, "You want some too darlin'?"

Once more Jessie raised her umbrella and, this time, with the pointed end, she repeatedly stabbed him in the groin with all her might. The buzzing insect had more of a sting this time and he bent over in agony, temporarily unable to do anything.

Jessie took this opportunity to help the woman up off the ground and back into her wheelchair, all the while being jostled by police who were busy assaulting other women.

She had just got the woman, who she later learned was called Rosa May Billingham and known as "the cripple suffragette", back into her chair when the policeman she had temporarily felled raised his truncheon and dealt Jessie a severe blow to the side of her head. She heard a sickening crack and fell to the ground unconscious.

He then turned his attention back to Miss Billingham and, still smarting from the stabbing of his testicles, he shoved his ugly, pock-marked face into hers and said, "Your turn now Missy, I've never had a cripple bitch before."

Rosa May tried to wheel herself away from him but he grabbed a hold of her chair and propelled her down an alley where a gang of men were hanging about. He bent down and said, "Looks like they'll do the job for me sweetheart, so I'll be getting back on duty." He then removed the rivets from her chair so she had no means of wheeling it and no means of escape.

Miss Billingham, who had no other option, faced the men with her head held high and asked, "Are you going to assault a crippled lady or are you going to help me? After all, it wouldn't be a fair fight, would it, five strong men and only me with legs that can't move?"

She must have connected with their better side since after muttering to each other for a few moments, one of them, obviously the gang leader, said, "Bert, you get the rivets back on this lady's wheelchair," then turning to Miss Billingham said, "we'll get you sorted Miss and move you to safety."

"Thank you," she said, "but a friend of mine is lying unconscious back there, she's seriously injured I think. That brute battered her head with his truncheon," she indicated Parliament Square, "would two of you please rescue her from further injury and get her to the nearest hospital?"

"Certainly Miss," replied the leader, "Fred, Alf, go and look for this lady's friend!"

BY THE TIME they found Jessie, Evangeline and Meg who had come across her at the same time, when coming from opposite directions, had managed to drag her to the edge of the thickest of the violence and they were kneeling beside her, white-faced and anxious.

Fred and Alf approached them and they started, fearing a new assault on them, but Fred held up his hand in a gesture of peace and said, "Don't be scared ladies," then pointing to Jessie, "this lady's friend sent us to help her and take her to hospital."

"We'll come with you," said a relieved Evangeline,

feeling these burly men would protect them from further abuse.

This hell, that Evangeline, Jessie and Meg had just miraculously escaped from, continued for six long hours. Women were repeatedly beaten and sexually assaulted. By evening, over two hundred women had been injured and over one hundred were arrested.

20

AFTERMATH

SATURDAY, 19TH NOVEMBER

The *Daily Mirror* printed a front page headline of, "Violent Scenes at Westminster". Below the headline was a very evocative photograph of Ada Wright, lying on the ground with her hands shielding her face whilst being towered over by policemen.

The image spoke for itself and, of course, the Government wanted it removed from circulation, with good reason. The Home Secretary, Winston Churchill, knowing what the suffragettes had planned, thanks to the wide distribution of their leaflets, as well as intelligence provided by Special Branch operatives, had called in thousands of extra policemen from forces in London, particularly the East End, who were instructed to "Do what you like to the women".

These policemen, who had to be at least five foot and ten inches to join the force, were used to dealing with fighting drunks and violent criminals and Churchill had let loose six thousand of them on three hundred unarmed women of all ages.

Number Ten Downing Street instigated an immediate cover-up and ordered the *Daily Mirror* to destroy the negatives of the image and to withdraw that edition of the newspaper from circulation. A little late, however, since several thousand copies had already been sold.

The proverbial cat was out of the bag and there was public shock and outrage. There were calls for a public enquiry into how this had been allowed to happen, but Churchill announced that there would be no formal government enquiry into the events of Friday the eighteenth of November 1910, which henceforth became known as "Black Friday".

Jessie Gilhooley had been taken to St Thomas's Hospital, just across the river from Westminster, where she was carefully examined and X-rayed and she was found to have sustained a fractured skull and was still unconscious. It would be some time before she would be well enough to travel back to Edinburgh.

Evangeline and Meg, looking like the walking wounded themselves, were very concerned as they sat at her bedside in the small, white single room, watching her pale, almost translucent face, as she breathed, in slow shallow breaths.

"Dae ye think she'll make a full recovery Evangeline?" asked Meg, "Ah jist cannae believe what happened yesterday. Ah dinnae ken what did happen other than we walked intae a wall o' brutal polis thugs."

"Well that's about the size of it Meg," Evangeline said, eyes not moving from Jessie. "It's obvious Churchill thought he would teach us a lesson. There must have been thousands of policemen willing to do us severe damage, not to mention those thugs they brought along to further molest us," she replied.

"Aye, but where did they come fae?" asked Meg, "surely there cannae be that many polis for Parlyment?"

"No Meg, there aren't," said Evangeline. "Most of them had Cockney accents and my guess is that they were brought in, especially, from the rougher parts of London, from the East End and the like, and their remit was to unleash the kind of brutality I've never seen before and never want to see again."

"Ah wonder what happened tae Jessie," said Meg, close to tears as she looked at her friend lying so still in the white bed, head bandaged.

"It seems that she tried to help a crippled woman in a wheelchair and a brute of a policeman hit her hard with his truncheon. At least, that's the story Bert and Alf told me."

They each fell silent as they tried to make sense of the events of the previous day. How many had ended up like Jessie? How much worse could it be than to have a fractured skull and hanging between life and death? They were startled from their dark thoughts by Jessie's weak voice.

"Oh Jessie!" cried Evangeline, "you're awake dearest girl. What did you say, it was so quiet that we didn't hear."

"Ah think Ah've lost ma umbrella," she repeated hoarsely.

"Don't you worry about that Jessie, I'll buy you five new umbrellas." said Evangeline, with relief.

"Oh Jessie," said Meg, "Ah'm that glad ye're awake, Ah'll go an' tell the nurse." and she got up and left the small room.

While they were waiting for Meg to come back, Evangeline sat holding Jessie's hand, stroking it affectionately. "I was so very worried about you Jess, I thought I was going to lose you and I couldn't live without you, my dearest girl."

Just then a doctor and nurse entered the room and Evangeline and Meg were asked to wait in the corridor while they examined Jessie.

When they came out, an anxious-looking Evangeline asked the doctor, "Is she going to be alright doctor? She will make a full recovery, won't she?"

"I think so Miss eh? ..." he said.

"Miss Frobisher," she replied.

"Yes, I think she will Miss Frobisher, at least I'm more confident of that now, although earlier this morning I thought it possible that she might not regain consciousness. That was a very nasty blow she received."

"Oh thank you doctor, thank you so much. How long will she have to stay in hospital?"

"I think at least two weeks, maybe more, it all depends on how she gets on. She will probably suffer from concussion for the next twenty-four hours or so, but we'll keep a close eye on her, Miss Frobisher, so try not to worry." He looked at his notes and said, "She was visiting from Edinburgh I see. Does she have any relatives here?"

"No, we all came down together a few days ago." She looked at Meg, including her in the party, "but my father is a Member of Parliament and has a flat in London, so I will stay on for a while, at least until she is well enough to travel home."

The doctor looked at Evangeline with new interest and nodded, "Ah yes, Sir Charles Frobisher."

Evangeline nodded and asked, "Do you know if there were many of the wounded at yesterday's deputation to Parliament, brought in here last night?"

He looked grim and said, "Yes, too many with contusions, broken noses and fractured and dislocated limbs I'm afraid."

"A truly awful experience for every woman there," Evangeline said.

"I know," the doctor replied, shaking his head, "my Aunt Ada was there yesterday and she was very badly abused by the police."

"I think I saw her being looked after by some friends," said Evangeline, then she added angrily, "Heads ought to roll for this, but I fear they won't."

The doctor just nodded and added, "You can go back in and see your friend now. Good day Miss Frobisher," and he hurried away to see his next patient.

Jessie was sleeping when they re-entered the room and they were glad to see that she had some colour in her cheeks now.

"Come Meg," said Evangeline, "we must go back to Amelia's and see how she fared yesterday, better than us I hope." I didn't see her after the police came charging at us and we all got split up."

"We should telephone Jean and tell her what's happened, put her mind at rest in case it's in the papers at hame," Meg suggested.

"Yes, we should," agreed Evangeline, "and I need to let my grandmother know that I'm alright, for the same reasons. I'll also have to grovel to my father and ask if I may use his flat," she said, then stopped suddenly and added, "damn it, I won't! I shall ask Amelia if I may remain at her house a while longer. What are you going to do Meg?"

"Ah'll have tae get hame, Ah cannae leave ma auld mother for any longer," she replied, "Ah'll jist collect ma bag and get a train hame this afternoon."

.   .   .

EVANGELINE WAVED Meg off at King's Cross station at three o'clock and then made her weary way to St Thomas's to visit Jessie. Amelia had fared better than Evangeline and Jessie but she had been arrested around five o'clock. She had told Evangeline and Meg that all of those arrested had been released without charge that morning. A sure sign of Churchill's complicity, Evangeline thought bitterly.

21

THAT SAME DAY
4 HATTON PLACE, EDINBURGH

W hilst the women were being battered and abused by the police and their ruffians in Parliament Square, Charles had been aboard the *Flying Scotsman* on his way home to Edinburgh from London, blissfully unaware of the horrors his daughter and all the other women were suffering.

The first he heard about it was on Saturday morning whilst he and Louisa were having breakfast. Maggie answered the the telephone and entered the morning room. "Sir John Sinclair is on the telephone for you Sir Charles," she announced.

Not expecting bad new, Charles wiped his mouth with his napkin, got up and went out into the hall. He was only gone a couple of minutes when he returned to the morning room ashen-faced.

Louisa was alarmed when she saw his grim expression. "What is it?" she whispered, fearing some awful news about Evangeline.

"Sir John has just had a telephone call from a colleague in London. Apparently the Home Secretary ordered a police presence of some six thousand to await the deputation of around three hundred or so suffragettes when they were marching on Parliament, yesterday, in protest at the failure of the Conciliation Bill," he said grimly. Louisa sat, now pale-faced herself, as he continued.

"Over two hundred women have been injured, some seriously and the reinforcements brought in from the East End and elsewhere, had been instructed to, and I quote Sir John, "Do what you want to them". Over a hundred women were arrested. What on earth was Churchill thinking?"

"Oh my God Charles!" said Louisa in horror," "Evangeline left for London on Thursday to be part of that deputation and we have no way of getting in touch with her to find out if she's safe or has been arrested."

"We shall just have to hope that she contacts Mother. It's usually Mother she telephones, not us. I must get my hands on a copy of that paper that Sinclair mentioned and see for myself. Sinclair said it had a photograph of a woman lying on the ground with her hands protecting her face, while policemen towered over her menacingly."

"How could such brutality be allowed to happen Charles?" Louisa asked fretfully.

"It's totally outrageous Louisa and there will have to be a public enquiry. As soon as I return to Westminster on Monday I shall be asking some very difficult questions," he promised.

"Mr Churchill has certainly taken his revenge for all the egg-throwing and bell-ringing, but such brutality! The man is nothing more than a tyrant with more power than conscience," she said angrily, "I can honestly say that he is the most hateful man and greatly discredits the Liberal Party and the Liberal Government."

"I can't disagree with you there, Louisa, most obnoxious," Charles replied.

"And I can't blame the woman who attacked him with a whip last year, I'm angry enough to want to do it myself," Louisa said, heatedly.

"Please calm yourself Louisa, let's wait until we read the report in the newspaper and hear from Evangeline," Charles said, soothingly.

"Will this stress and strain never end Charles?" she asked, shaking her head wearily.

"I suspect not until women are granted the vote, my dear," he replied. "I'm just going to drive into town and get a copy of the *Daily Mirror*, they sell it at the news stand on the corner of the High Street and George IV Bridge. I won't be long." He kissed her on the cheek and hurried out. Louisa sat, deep in anxious thought, for a very long time.

CHARLES WAS ACTUALLY AWAY LONGER than he had intended since a thought struck him as he drove up the High Street. "Since I'm in the area," he said to himself, "I shall pay a visit to the WSPU office in Drummond Street. Hopefully there will be someone there who will be able to give me some information on the situation."

He parked and jumped out of the car, a few yards down from the news vendor, and quickly bought a copy of the *Daily Mirror*. He stopped in his tracks as he looked at the photograph on the front page. "Good Lord!" he exclaimed under his breath, taking in the story the image told, "this is very serious indeed."

He got into the car and drove the short distance along Chambers Street and up South Bridge to Drummond Street.

He stopped the car in front of the WSPU office and was relieved to see that there were lights on inside and he could see women moving about in the front office.

He rang the doorbell and it was opened by Jean Kennedy, who he recognised from the incident at the Queen's Hall in January.

"Yes?" she asked, "can I help you?"

"Please may I come in? I'm Evangeline Frobisher's father," he said.

She stood back, allowing him to enter and said, "Evangeline isn't here, she's in London."

"Yes, I know," he replied. "I was wondering whether you can throw any light on this?" he held out the newspaper for her to see.

"Come into the office and I'll tell you what we know so far," Jean, who normally used the vernacular, was in professional mode, especially when speaking to "the enemy" i.e. a member of the Liberal Government.

He followed her into the front office and he was impressed by the professional and organised layout, as well as the industry going on, even on a Saturday morning.

She introduced him to the two women who were busy putting letters into envelopes, then said, "Please take a seat Sir Charles."

She began, "On my way into the office this morning, I saw the *Mirror's* headlines with that photograph and I bought a copy. As soon as I arrived here, I telephoned Head Office at Clement's Inn." She stopped and shuddered, thinking about what she had been told, then went on, "Around three to four hundred women marched to Parliament Square in protest at the failure of the Conciliation Bill and to present a petition demanding the vote." She paused again, an expression of disbelief and shock on her face.

"Go on," Charles urged gently.

"It was a peaceful protest and an orderly deputation, although they were expecting the House of Commons police to make a few arrests, as is the precedent, but when they rounded the corner into Parliament Square, they were met by thousands of policemen who immediately began attacking the women with their fists and truncheons. Even elderly women were abused, with many being hurled into a hostile mob of bystanders who then threw them onto the ground."

She paused and looked at Charles, a mixture of anger and embarrassment on her expressive face, then she forced herself to go on. Charles sat grim-faced as he listened to her.

"It wasn't just physical violence, you understand, the police were also sexually assaulting the women, even ripping their underclothes. Do you realise that the women were trapped there, surrounded by the police, as the assault on them went on for six hours?"

Charles put his head in his hands for a few moments and then looked at Jean and asked, "Have you any news of Evangeline?"

"I'm afraid not, there were over 100 arrests and many women were injured and not accounted for. We're hoping to hear more this afternoon."

Just at that moment the telephone rang and Jean said, "Excuse me, I must take this call, it may be more news."

Charles nodded and watched her intently as she listened to the person on the other end of the phone. He thought he saw a look of relief and she said, "At least that is something," then she asked, "Do you have any news of Evangeline Frobisher, Jessie Gilhooley or Meg McIntyre?" She looked grim as she replied, "I see, alright I'll await further news. Thank you, goodbye."

She put down the receiver and looked grimly at Charles. "They have released everyone they arrested, without charge, so you can read into that what you will. Evangeline, Jessie and Meg were not among those arrested and they think it's possible that they may have been taken to hospital. They're making enquiries now." Charles looked stricken and, feeling sorry for him, she hurried to reassure him.

"I'm told it was utter mayhem and many of the injured women made it back to Clement's Inn. Perhaps Evangeline and the others made it to the safety of the house where they were staying."

"Thank you Miss eh?" although he recognised her, he didn't remember her name in his agitated state.

"Miss Kennedy," she helped him out, "Jean Kennedy."

"Thank you Miss Kennedy, you have been very helpful and, from what you have told me and what I have seen in this," he tapped the photograph on the front page of the *Daily Mirror*, "I am outraged at what appears to be extreme and heavy-handed actions by the police and I can assure you that when I return to the Commons on Monday, I shall be calling for a public enquiry into yesterday's events." He got up and shook Jean's hand, nodded to the other two women and said, "Good morning ladies and thank you."

Jean showed him to the door and when she returned to the front office, she said, "Well, I think we might have misjudged the Honourable Sir Charles Frobisher."

Mary, one of the two women there and always mistrustful of men, said, "We'll see whether his words become deeds, aye, time will tell."

22

HATTON PLACE

A LITTLE LATER

By the time Charles returned to Hatton Place, Louisa had some mixed news for him.

"Charles you've been gone ages, where have you been?" she asked, partly relieved at his arrival and partly annoyed by his lengthy absence, considering he had only gone out for a newspaper.

"I'm so sorry Louisa, I was so anxious for news about Evangeline that I went to the office in Drummond Street to see if they had any news of her," he replied, "but they haven't heard, either from, or, about her."

"I have some news Charles, your mother has just telephoned. Evangeline called her about twenty minutes ago."

"Is she alright?" Charles asked.

"Sit down Charles and I'll tell you what she told your mother," replied Louisa. Sitting on the sofa next to him, she said, "Evangeline said she was alright, just a few bruises and the same goes for Meg McIntyre ..." she began, but Charles interrupted her.

"Do you think she was telling the truth or just not wanting to worry Mother?"

"I think the fact that she was able to telephone your mother is testimony that she is, more or less, alright," replied Louisa, trying not to lose her patience, "shall I go on?"

"Yes, of course. Sorry Louisa," he said, apologetically.

She smiled at him, accepting the apology, then said, "It's Jessie Gilhooley that they're worried about, she's in St Thomas's hospital with a fractured skull. Apparently, a policeman hit her hard on the side of the head with his truncheon as she was trying to help a crippled woman that he - said policeman - had tipped out of her wheelchair onto the ground." She looked at him in shocked disbelief, "Really Charles, the police force is meant to protect the public, not beat them up."

"I know Louisa, but the information coming from the WSPU head office is worse than that. Many, many women were also sexually assaulted and thrown by police into a crowd of tough male bystanders, probably incited by Special Branch, who were told they could do what they liked to them. I think it has to be the most appalling thing I've ever heard."

Louisa looked stricken, "Oh my Lord Charles!" she said as a thought struck her, "do you think that happened to Evangeline too?"

"I don't know my dear, but from what Miss Kennedy told me, in Drummond Street, the police seem to have revelled in their violence against unarmed women on a peaceful march," and he added, "I have sworn to call for a full public enquiry into the appalling events of yesterday, as soon as I return to the House on Monday." He got up and began to pace up and down the drawing room, "I promise you Louisa, that snake Churchill is not going to slither away from this, this ... atrocity."

He was silent for a few moments, pacing all the while, then he asked, "Is Evangeline coming home soon?"

"No, she has decided to stay on in London until Jessie is well enough to travel home. Meg McIntyre is coming back later today as she has an elderly mother to look after."

"Do you think she'll stay at the flat with me?" he asked, tentatively.

"From what your mother said, she'll be staying with Amelia Wainwright, that's the friend from university who was accommodating them whilst they were in London," Louisa told him.

Disappointed, he said, "I suppose it was too much to hope for." He sighed, feeling dreadfully tired with all that he had learned over the past couple of hours. "Ah well, I'd better contact some colleagues, see if I can drum up support for getting an enquiry under way."

"Good luck Charles. I won't be in for lunch, I'm meeting Mother, Letty and your mother for lunch in Jenners' Garden Room and I'm not looking forward to telling them the news." She kissed him on the cheek and went upstairs to get ready, for her outing, with mixed emotions. On the one hand, she was dreading telling them about all that had taken place at Westminster yesterday, but on the other, it would be good to have the support of the three women she loved and trusted most in the world.

23

PLATFORM 1, WAVERLEY STATION
THAT EVENING

T he King's Cross train was due in at nine o'clock in the evening and Meg Couldn't wait to get home and have a long soak in the old zinc bath. Her shoulder, although not actually dislocated as she'd first thought, was giving her considerable pain and her bruised body ached from continually being grabbed by rough hands and thrown to the ground.

It was a wonder that neither she, nor Evangeline, had any broken bones and they had both been examined by one of the doctors on duty while Jessie was receiving emergency treatment.

As the train puffed its way into the Waverley Station, she stood up wearily and reached for her bag, wincing at the pain any movement seemed to cause. She planned on taking laudanum and hoped for a healing night's sleep, once she'd seen to her frail, widowed and elderly mother.

As the only unmarried woman in the McIntyre family, as was so often the case then, it fell to Meg to be the one to remain in the family home and look after her mother. However, she had put her foot down and insisted that she would not be giving up her WSPU work and that her sisters-in-law must be drafted in to help, especially when she had to be away overnight. This had been a hard-won battle, she reflected now, as she wondered what her brothers would say about her experiences in London. But she had been a suffragist for so many years that she guarded her independence jealously, even though she was tied to the care of her mother.

The train slowed down and came to a halt at Platform 1. She waited for the guard to open the door as she had no strength left to pull down the heavy window and lean out to reach the door handle. She wasn't looking forward to the steep walk up Market Street to the Lawnmarket, where the McIntyre's lived in a small second floor flat.

To her total astonishment a great cheer went up as she stepped onto the platform and Jean Kennedy, accompanied by a dozen suffragettes, came towards her, clapping their hands in welcome and admiration.

Jean embraced her and she winced slightly, then Jean stood back, holding her gently by the arms now and said, "Oh Meg, Ah'm sorry, Ah didnae realise how sair ye must be. Let me take yer bag for ye."

"It's a'right Jean, Ah'm jist a wee bit fragile the now, but the bruising will soon heal."

The others came up and shook her hand gently, saying," Welcome home Meg and well done!"

"It's good tae be back, but a' Ah want right now is tae get hame and see ma mother and then have a long soak in the bath," she said, "so Ah'd better make a start on Market Street and the steep trail up Bank Street, Ah'm nearly sleeping oan ma feet, ye ken, it's been an awfy tirin' couple o' days."

"There's no way we're lettin' ye walk hame Meg, we've a'

clubbed thegither an' Ah'm takin' ye hame in a cab," Jean told her.

She burst into tears with relief and the stress of the past thirty-six hours. Jean put her arm around her and led her along the platform to the station exit. The others all called "Goodbye" and sent their best wishes for a good, restful night's sleep.

"Come on Meg," said Jean, "let's get you transport fit for a heroine. Ye can tell me a' aboot Jessie and Evangeline on the way."

Sunday afternoon

AFTER SEEING to her mother the previous night, Jessie had a soothing bath with some lavender oil. She then took a laudanum powder with a medicinal drop of brandy and she fell into a deep and dreamless sleep.

She did not waken up until nine o'clock on Sunday morning and she was pleasantly surprised to find that her aches and pains had subsided somewhat, although her shoulder was still sore and her bruises tender.

She got her mother up and dressed and made a breakfast of porridge and toast for them both. She was just clearing away the dishes when there was a knock on the door of the flat.

Wondering who it could be at this time on a Sunday morning, she opened it to find Sir Charles Frobisher standing there. She hadn't seen him since she had thrown eggs at him earlier in the year.

He removed his hat and, as though he knew what she

was thinking, she thought she saw a fleeting twinkle in his eyes. "I'm so sorry to turn up unannounced Miss McIntyre," he began, "but I shall be returning to London later today and I wondered whether I might ask you a few questions regarding the events in Parliament Square on Friday. I understand from Miss Kennedy that you were there with my daughter, Evangeline and Mrs Gilhooley, who was seriously injured."

Meg looked behind her, at the still untidy kitchen and she wasn't sure whether to let him in or not. Charles, reading her indecision correctly, said gently and persuasively, "I'm not here to make any judgements on your home, I must reassure you, but I think it would greatly help the women, who were so badly treated on Friday, if you would agree to talk to me." He smiled his wonderful, engaging smile that had given his patients implicit trust in him when he was a doctor.

Meg returned the smile, opened the door wide and said, "Come ben the hoose Sir Charles, it's no' very tidy since Ah didnae get hame until late last night."

"Thank you, Miss McIntyre," Charles said and followed her into a warm, cosy kitchen where Mrs McIntyre was sitting at the table, her sewing in her hands.

She looked up at the stranger and then at Meg, a question in her old rheumy eyes. Meg said, "Ma, ye ken ma pals Jessie and Evangeline, don't ye?" The old woman nodded, "well this is Evangeline's father and he'd like a wee word wi' me aboot Friday's demonstration."

Her mother knew she was involved in an organisation campaigning for votes for women, but her knowledge or understanding didn't go any further than that, nor had Meg apprised her of the militant acts she had been involved in.

"Oh aye hen. Hello Sir," she said, nodding, "Ah'll go ben the hoose an' let ye speak tae the gentleman in peace." She reached for her walking stick, eased herself up from the table and made her slow way to the door. "Bring ma sewin' will ye Meg," she said as she reached the door to the adjoining bedroom.

When Meg returned, she filled the kettle and put it on the gas cooker. "Would ye like a cup o' tea Sir Charles? Ah'm in need o' one, so Ah'm makin' a pot anyway," she said.

"That would be most welcome Miss McIntyre," he replied, "may I sit down?"

"Please do. Ah'm sorry, Ah dinnae ken where ma manners are, it must be the effects o' the last few days," she said, as she cleared the breakfast dishes from the table.

While Meg busied herself making the tea, Charles said, "I believe you endured the most awful and shocking experiences on Friday, outside Parliament."

She was silent as she poured the boiling water onto the warmed tea leaves, stirred it briskly and then set it on the table. After she'd put cups and saucers on the table she sat down and finally replied.

"Aye, Ah've had better experiences at the dentist," she said with a humourless laugh. "What is it ye wid like me tae tell ye?" she asked him, deadly serious now.

"It is my intention to ask the Home Secretary to instigate a full enquiry into the actions of the police on duty at Westminster on Friday. I further intend to be on the committee that will undertake the enquiry and, as part of that process, as many women as possible who were there will need to be interviewed and give statements on what they experienced there or on what they witnessed," he said, gravely.

"So it's no' gonnae be swept under the carpet then?" Meg

asked, surprised at the stance of this Liberal MP and Cabinet Minister.

"Not if I have anything to do with it Miss McIntyre," Charles replied, "I may not agree with the militant acts that my daughter and, yourself perhaps are involved in, but I will not tolerate criminal and violent acts being perpetrated by the very people who are meant to protect the public. I want to know who is responsible for ordering such behaviour by those policemen who were on duty that day."

"Ah see," she said. "Ask me anything ye want, Ah'll dae ma best tae help ye."

"Thank you," replied Charles, taking a notebook and pencil from the inside pocket of his jacket. "Please tell me what happened from the time you left Caxton Hall until you arrived in Parliament Square."

Meg described the peaceful procession from Caxton Street to Westminster.

"And what happened when you got there?"

"Well the three o' us, that is Evangeline, Jessie an' masel', were maybe twenty or so rows back an' all of a sudden the procession stopped an' we could hear shoutin' an' screamin' ahead. We hadnae a clue as tae what wis goin' on, but bit by bit, we started movin' again an' as we turned the corner, that's when we saw what was happenin'," she recalled, eyes wide with the horror of it.

"In your own words Miss McIntyre, what was happening?"

"The polis were chargin' intae the women, punchin' some in the face, hittin' others wi' their truncheons," she said. "One minute we were a' thegither an' the next Ah couldnae see Jessie or Evangeline. They seemed tae have been swallowed up in a sea o'polis an' we were surrounded. There wis nae goin' forwards an' nae goin' back, jist gettin' tossed fae pillar tae post, as it were." She stopped, the memory of the events overwhelming her. She lifted her teacup with trembling hands and took a few sips of the, now cooling, liquid. It seemed to revive her, since when Charles asked, "Do you feel able to continue Miss McIntyre, or have you had enough for one day?"

She replied, "Naw, let's get this over an' done wi'."

She told him about her own personal experiences of abuse and assault by the police and bystanders, and of the awful moment when they found Jessie unconscious on the ground and the help of the men in getting them all safely to the hospital, away from what felt like a war zone.

When she had recounted her tale of the events of Black Friday, Charles put his notebook and pencil back in his jacket pocket. He said, "Thank you so much Miss McIntyre for your assistance and for sharing those very difficult experiences with me. Should you have need of it, my wife works in the High Street police station counselling female victims of serious crime and assault." He read the look on her face and added, "Even if the assault was caused by police, it wasn't the Edinburgh police force. Just know that it is there, should you want to avail yourself of the service."

"Thank you, Ah wis aware o' Evangeline's mother's work an' Ah will think aboot it."

He got up to leave, picked his hat up from the chair where he'd laid it when he came into the room and said, "I shall leave you and your mother in peace now."

She nodded and said, "Ah'll see ye tae the door."

At the door, he shook her hand and said, "I hope you have a speedy recovery from all your injuries and trauma."

"Thank you Sir Charles, and Ah'm sorry aboot the egg on yer jacket," she said, a little shame-faced.

Charles actually laughed and said, "You were only doing your job Miss McIntyre."

He turned and went down the stairs and Meg stood for a long time, thinking of everything that had happened in the past seventy-two hours. Eventually, she gave herself a mental shake and went in to see how her mother was doing in the bedroom.

THE CHAMBER, HOUSE OF COMMONS

MONDAY, 21ST NOVEMBER 1910

After various Corporation Bills had been discussed, the Speaker of the House, John Lowther, opened the floor for any questions. So far, the subject of the events of the previous Friday was conspicuous by its absence.

"Sir Charles Frobisher," said the Speaker.

Charles was on his feet in a fraction of a second, "Thank you Mr Speaker. Will the Home Secretary instigate a full Government enquiry into the shocking violence, perpetrated by the police, that took place here outside this House, on Friday last?"

Winston Churchill stood up as Charles sat down. "I have no intention of instigating an enquiry since there are insufficient grounds and there is no need to waste Parliamentary time and resources to do so. Instead, I shall be writing to the Chief Constable of the Metropolitan Police and that will be sufficient." The Home Secretary sat down again.

Charles immediately got to his feet and asked, "As yet, we do not know the exact numbers, but from the information I have gathered so far, many, many women were physically and sexually assaulted by members of the Metropolitan Police, many requiring hospital treatment and I personally know of one who sustained a fractured skull after being hit by a policeman's truncheon. Are you seriously telling this House Sir, that those actions by the police, heavy-handed, at best, and criminal at worst, do not constitute sufficient grounds to initiate an enquiry?" Charles sat down again.

"Shame! Shame!" from some members who were supporters of women's suffrage.

Churchill stood up again and replied, "I am sure that my Right Honourable friend must realise that, with Parliament closing in one week's time for the General Election, there are more pressing matters that the Government must give its attention to." He sat down, indicating that the matter was closed.

Charles stood up again and said, "I respectfully suggest that the safety of the public is an important matter for His Majesty's Government, and the Home Secretary in particular, to grant time after the election, to allow a full public enquiry into the events of Friday, the eighteenth of November."

Churchill stood up and said, "Mr Speaker, I have given the Honourable gentleman my answer and that is final." He then picked up his papers and left the Chamber..

Charles sat down, feeling deflated and defeated.

Later, as Charles left the Chamber, he was approached by a journalist called Henry Brailsford, who Charles knew as an acquaintance and fellow supporter of women's suffrage. Brailsford had founded the Men's League for Women's Suffrage and had resigned from his position on the *Daily News* in 1909 when the paper supported the forcible feeding of hunger-striking suffragettes in prison.

"I was in the public gallery when you called for a full public enquiry and I'm sorry that Churchill has decided to dodge the issue," he said to Charles after the two men had shaken hands. "Can we go somewhere less public to talk? I have an idea and a proposition for you."

Charles regarded Brailsford thoughtfully and nodded, "Of course, let's go into my private office, we won't be disturbed there." He knew the man to be left of centre in his political views, but he respected his principles.

Once in his office, Charles said, "Please do sit down, Mr Brailsford. This violence to the suffragettes on Friday last is a bad business, a bad business indeed. Now tell me about this proposition."

"I agree wholeheartedly and would ideally like a member of the government, that is yourself and some members of the all party Conciliation Committee, to undertake the enquiry that Churchill is refusing to commit to," he said, regarding Charles and trying to assess what his response would be.

Charles was thoughtful for several moments. He was certainly disappointed by the Home Secretary's outright rejection of an enquiry into the events of the eighteenth, but he was unsure whether he ought to get involved so close to a General Election.

Eventually, he said, "My own daughter was caught up in the violence and, although I have not yet seen her, a friend of hers suffered a fractured skull, as you, no doubt, heard me say in the Chamber earlier. I'm hoping to speak to her personally later today, I have already taken a statement from the third woman in the deputation that travelled from Edinburgh and who returned home on Saturday."

"Excellent!" said Brailsford, enthusiastically, "I have spoken to the other members of the Conciliation Committee, just this morning, and it has been agreed that we interview the women who were caught up in the violence, or at least, as many as are willing to provide us with evidence."

"I shall let you have my notes from yesterday's interview, but such is the nature of some of the assaults, that it might be difficult for the women to bring themselves to speak of it," said Charles.

"Yes, I realise that, Sir Charles," Brailsford replied, "so I have asked Dr Jessie Murray, who is a suffragette herself, if she will come with me to conduct the interviews. This will take some time to complete and it will probably be some time into the new year before we can submit the report to the Home Office. The General Election will be well and truly over by then and there will be no excuse for Churchill to refuse time for it, if he retains his seat, that is."

"Oh, he will, no doubt," replied Charles, "but possibly with a reduced majority. By the way, just call me Charles, not Sir."

"Thank you Charles, I'm Henry," said Brailsford. "I'll get back to you when I have something to report, but, as I said, it'll most likely be into the new year."

"I shall do what I can to get some of my colleagues on board, although that will have to wait until after the election," said Charles. "In the meantime, thank you for getting in touch and if I do manage to get a statement from my daughter's friend later today, I will forward a copy to you."

The two men shook hands and, after Brailsford left, Charles sat for a long time, deep in thought.

MEANWHILE, not far from Westminster, Evangeline was sitting at Jessie's bedside, holding her hand gently in hers.

Jessie was now beginning to recover from the concussion and was feeling much better, although it would still be some time before she would be fit enough to be discharged and make the journey back to Edinburgh.

"You're certainly looking a lot better Jessie," said Evangeline, "I can't tell you how scared I was that you wouldn't regain consciousness."

"Ah must be made o' strong stuff Evie," said Jessie, smiling fondly at her friend, "and Ah can tell ye that if it had been the other way roond and it had been you lyin' here Ah'd be worried tae."

Evangeline smiled, gratified that her affection for Jessie was being reciprocated. Stroking Jessie's hand now, she said, "Jessie dear, I need to tell you that I am very fond of you. Ever since that brute of a husband hurt you I've felt very protective of you and, over the past twelve months, our friendship has deepened ..." she trailed off, unsure how to go on.

"Ah ken what ye're tryin' tae say Evie," Jessie rescued her, "because Ah feel exactly the same. Ah didnae ken it wis possible tae feel sae close tae another wummin, but that brute, as ye called him, actually did me a favour that day." She blushed, feeling a little shy to be putting her growing feelings for Evangeline into words. "Ah've become very fond o' ye Evie an' Ah ken this kind o' thing isnae conventional, but Ah think you feel the same way aboot me, unless Ah've got it a' wrong?" She looked up, a trace of worry on her face.

Evangeline smiled and actually laughed with relief and sheer happiness. She stroked Jessie's hand affectionately and said, "No Jess, you haven't got it wrong, my darling girl but, as you said, it isn't a conventional kind of relationship, at least not in Edinburgh circles, so we may have to take things slowly and not bring any unwanted attention to ourselves. Now I think I should go and let you rest or the nurse will be chasing me away."

Jessie was smiling widely and said, "Oh Evie, Ah am glad ye said a' that and, despite havin' an awfy headache, Ah'm that happy."

Evangeline got up and kissed her gently on the lips. "Get well soon Jess, so I can take you home."

"Ah will Evie," she replied and lay back on her pillows with a big, contented sigh.

Despite the events of the previous few days Evangeline suddenly felt her heart and spirits soaring. "Everything is going to be alright," she thought to herself.

25

DECEMBER 1910

4 HATTON PLACE

The results of the General Election in December almost repeated those in January, with the Liberal Government remaining in power, but only with the support of the Irish National Party.

A tentative truce had been tacitly agreed between Charles and Evangeline after the shocking violence of Black Friday. Evangeline's opinion of her father began to change when she discovered that he he not only interviewed Meg in Edinburgh and had visited Jessie in hospital, but also had asked Churchill to conduct a public enquiry into the brutal actions and behaviour of the police. She was even more gratified to hear that he was to be part of the Brailsford-led enquiry by the all-party Conciliation Committee.

Jessie was discharged from St Thomas's hospital and brought home to Lauder Road, with Charlotte's agreement, so that she could convalesce under Evangeline's care.

Christmas Day at the Frobishers in Hatton Place was a much happier affair than it had been in several years, due mainly to the mutual tolerance of each other's positions by Evangeline and her father. Louisa was so happy that she decided to have a proper celebration for her family and friends.

Around the middle of December, as she and Charles were having a drink before supper in their cosy drawing room, she told Charles about her idea.

"Charles, I was thinking of having a big Christmas dinner for all of our families and friends, now that relations between you and Evangeline have improved so much, what do you think?"

"I think that would be very nice Louisa dear, who were you thinking of inviting?" he asked, smiling at her fondly. Louisa had always loved Christmas time and he had been vexed at how saddened she had been over recent Christmases.

"Well, Mother and Father, of course, and your mother and Evangeline," she began to list, on her fingers, the guests she would invite, "Letty and Wilf, and Rose, we can't leave poor Rose out now that she's on her own, and we can't leave Jessie out either, since she's been staying with your mother. Oh and maybe Mary, as she's like a daughter to Rose with them both being very active in the Women's Freedom League." She stopped abruptly, seeing that he was laughing. "What's so funny Charles?" she asked, puzzled.

"You are my darling," he replied kindly. "You are an incorrigible hostess Louisa, and you're almost babbling with the excitement of it all. I do so love you," he said, going over and kissing her fondly.

"But how is Maggie going to cope with so many people? She manages just - when it is us and Mother, or your parents." he replied, thoughtfully. After Mrs Hammond retired, some years before, Maggie was promoted to the position of housekeeper under the careful guidance of Louisa.

"I've thought of that Charles, and I'll ask Mother if Cook and Minnie can come and help out, in fact, some of the cooking could be done in Heriot Row and transported here on Christmas morning," she said, pleased to have it all so well thought out and organised.

"I suppose that would work, as long as your Mother and her staff are agreeable."

"Oh they will be Charles," she replied confidently, "Cook's motto is 'the more the merrier'. Remember some of the dinner parties Mother hosted for Father's legal friends and colleagues?"

"Yes, alright," he said, hands up in an exaggerated act of surrender, "I do and I'm sure our Christmas party will be a total success."

Just then, Maggie knocked on the door, came into the room and said, "Supper is served Lady Frobisher, Sir Charles."

"Thank you Maggie," Louisa replied, "we'll be along presently."

26

CHRISTMAS DAY 1910

S unday, the twenty-fifth of December dawned crisp and bright and Charles drove his mother and Louisa to St Giles for the Christmas service. Afterwards, they and other members of the congregation stood outside chatting happily and wishing each other "Merry Christmas!" before returning home.

Back in Hatton Place, Louisa made a final inspection of the dining room to make sure everything was in order. She nodded, pleased with the table decorations that she and Charles's mother had made one pleasant afternoon the previous week, while Rosie, Charlotte's elderly lurcher, lay snoozing and dreaming in front of the morning room fire.

From the dining room, she went into the large drawing room at the front of the house. She breathed in the fragrance of the seasonal pot-pourri with its sharp hint of cloves.

Charles entered the room at that moment, and Louisa said, "Oh Charles, doesn't it look so lovely and festive?"

They stood admiring the large fir tree festooned with colourful sparkling garlands and glass baubles, but their pride and joy this Christmas was the set of electric tree lights, in red, green and gold, which Charles had brought home from London as a special surprise for Louisa. They hadn't told anyone about them and they were looking forward to surprising their guests, Charles would switch them on when they were having their pre-dinner sherry. Louisa was almost child-like in her excitement and Charles loved her all the more for it. They had spent the previous evening decorating the drawing room and dressing the tree.

The fire was blazing in the large grate and the soft wall lights seemed to flicker, reflecting the flames. Along the top of the marble mantlepiece, a long green garland lay with gold pines cones positioned at regular intervals, and the gilt-edged mirror above it gave the room the appearance of being twice its size.

"It's lovely Louisa," Charles said, taking her hand in his, "You and Mother have done a wonderful job. Shall we light the candles now?"

"Yes, please do Charles, I do so love Christmas," she replied, smiling happily.

They looked around the lovely room, glowing with candlelight and firelight when the doorbell rang. Louisa and Charles went into the vestibule to greet their first guests, as Maggie opened the door to Louisa's parents, Lord and Lady Moncrieff.

"Happy Christmas Mother, Happy Christmas Father," Louisa greeted and kissed them.

"Happy Christmas Louisa!" both of her parents said at the same time.

Charles kissed his mother-in law's cheek and shook hands with his father-in-law and they exchanged festive greetings.

"May I take your coats and hats Lord and Lady Moncrieff?" asked Maggie in her best manner.

After giving Maggie their outdoor things, they all went into the drawing room and Charles poured sherry for them all.

Charles's mother followed a few minutes later with Rosie who was sporting a new red velvet collar. She followed her mistress into the drawing room and lay by her feet while the humans talked excitedly around her. She didn't see what all the fuss was about, but she enjoyed the extra attention and any tasty morsels given to her by the doting friends and family of her mistress.

"Aren't Evangeline and Jessie with you Mother?" asked Charles when they hadn't followed Charlotte into the drawing room.

"They'll be along shortly Charles," she said, "Evangeline was still wrapping gifts, would you believe, on Christmas morning?" she tutted good-naturedly.

Letty and Wilf were next to arrive, with arms full of gifts for everyone and, after Charles had placed them under the Christmas tree, he poured them each a sherry.

The remaining guests, Rose, Mary, Evangeline and Jessie arrived at the same time and they were chattering away like magpies while Maggie took their hats and coats and hung them in the cloakroom. She didn't resent her friend, Rose, being a guest while she waited on her, since Rose had come up in the world since their early days when they were both housemaids.

Once everyone had a glass in their hands, Charles went over to the Christmas tree, and called for everyone's attention. "Ladies and gentlemen," he announced. Everyone in the room turned towards him and, as one, they gasped in delighted surprise as he switched on the lights.

There were "Oohs" and "Ah's" from the guests and Louisa and Charles beamed at each other.

"A toast," said Charles, raising his sherry glass, "Merry Christmas everyone and may 1911 be healthy and prosperous for you all."

"Merry Christmas!" chorused the guests, "and a Happy New Year!"

Just then, Maggie entered the drawing room and announced, "Dinner is served ladies and gentlemen."

Maggie didn't mind working on Christmas day as it was traditional for the working classes in Scotland to observe Hogmanay rather than Christmas. She was, however, looking forward to the traditional gifts from her employers on Boxing Day.

After the sumptuous feast, everybody returned to the drawing room for the exchanging of gifts, games and conversation. They were all in good spirits and full of seasonal goodwill.

The guests belonged to four different organisations, all wanting votes for women, and as is often the case at this kind of gathering, they had split into a small male group and a larger female one. The proverbial fly on the wall, hovering near either group, might have heard the following snippets of conversation.

The Ladies

EVANGELINE SAID, "I know that every person in this room wants women to have the vote." She looked at her mother, Aunt Letty and grandmothers, in turn, and added, "Some of you have been campaigning for decades, long before I was born and I know the male contingent over there," she looked across the room at her father, grandfather and Uncle Wilf, "are all supporters of female suffrage. I just want to say that I appreciate that and want to acknowledge that we are all going about achieving that goal in our own different ways. Today, I'm especially glad that we have been able to set those different ways aside in order to enjoy Christmas 1910."

"Well said Evangeline," said her mother, applauding her.

"Hear! Hear!" replied her grandmother Frobisher.

The Gentlemen

AT THE OTHER side of the large room the men were talking politics.

"Honestly James," Charles said to his father-in-law, "the House of Lords have too much power, you know, and they're not even elected. There are too many Conservatives in that elite chamber, wouldn't you agree?"

Lord Moncrieff, who only rarely took his seat in the Lords due to his commitments in the High Court, replied, "I agree wholeheartedly Charles, especially when they're thwarting legislation to help the poorest in society. I'm talking about the "People's Budget", that we tried to introduce in 1909 to raise taxes to fund social welfare programmes for the poor but the Conservative members of the Lords sunk the damn thing."

"Well, the General Election hasn't exactly given us the mandate we need, so we'll have to ask the King for permission to increase the number of Liberal peers in the Lords to get the Bill passed," said Charles.

"Do you think he will?" asked Wilf, speaking for the first time, "I mean allow you to create more Liberal peers?"

"That remains to be seen," said Charles, with little hope in his voice.

"Well, if it will help, Charles," Lord Moncrieff interjected, "I shall have to make it my business to be in the Lords for the Bill when it comes before us and I will canvass as many colleagues as I can, see if I can persuade them to vote for it."

The Ladies

"AND HOW ARE you feeling now Jessie?" Louisa asked Evangeline's friend.

"I'm a lot better now, thank you for asking Lady Frobisher," Jessie replied shyly. "Dr Cunningham," she looked at Letty, "has been monitoring my progress and I should be back in the office early in the New Year."

And so, the conversations ran on until it began to grow dark outside and, every now and again, Charles would leave James and Wilf in conversation while he put more logs on the fire. As he did so, he would catch Louisa's eye and the familiar affectionate look would pass between them.

At five o'clock, Lady Moncrieff said, "Louisa dear, on behalf of your father and me, I want to thank you for a lovely day, for the great company and delicious food, but we must be going home now."

As she said it, she glanced at the window and saw big, thick snowflakes falling. "Look everyone!" she said, "we're having a white Christmas after all."

The younger women hurried across the room to the window and looked out. "Look Mother," said Evangeline, "it's starting to lie thickly already." Then, turning to Jessie and her grandmother, she said, "Jessie, Grammie, we'll have to wrap up warmly, it looks like it's freezing out there."

By this time, the men had stopped talking and they too were looking at the thickly falling snow.

"I'll drive you all home Mother," offered Charles.

"We can fit you all into our car," said Letty. "We're going in that direction anyway Charles, no point in you going out in this weather."

"Nonsense!" exclaimed Charlotte, "it isn't far and we'll enjoy the brisk walk, won't we Rosie?" she said to her loyal lurcher, "and you can wear the coat that Louisa gave you for Christmas."

Amongst the presents under the tree was a waterproof coat with a velvet-trimmed collar that Louisa had ordered especially for Rosie. As if to show her appreciation she went over to Louisa, tail wagging enthusiastically.

Soon all the guests were huddled in their warm outdoor coats and hats and Louisa and Charles stood inside their doorway, saying their goodbyes.

Once inside again, he put his arm around Louisa's shoulder and said, "Well my dear, that was a most pleasant Christmas Day, the very best in recent years. Well done!"

"It was wonderful, wasn't it Charles?" she asked, as they went back into the warm drawing room and she watched the little coloured lights on the Christmas tree, brighter now that it was dark outside. Then she added in a dreamy voice, "I would go as far as to say it was magical."

They sat on the sofa for a long time, just holding hands, in the soft candlelight and firelight.

27

EARLY NEW YEAR, 1911

enry Brailsford and Dr Jessie Murray undertook the investigation into the violence on Black Friday and began interviewing witnesses and victims who were there on the day.

The evidence was divided into categories, including one entitled, "Torture and Indecent Conduct", which speaks to the shocking and violent behaviour of the police.

When all the evidence had been collected, they found that individual statements contained reports of more than one type of violence or offence. In the margins of the written evidence there was a code which related to the different categories, as follows.

"A = ACTS of violence
    AI = Methods of Torture
    B = Indecent Conduct [assault]
    D = After effects of treatment received
    E = References to plain-clothes detectives
    F = Improper language of police

J = Police numbers"

TWO WOMEN DIED in the aftermath of Black Friday. Mary Clarke was Emily Pankhurst's sister and her death had been attributed to Black Friday and what she suffered in the days following it. She died of a brain haemorrhage on Christmas Day 1910. The other woman was called Henria Williams, who'd had a weak heart. In her evidence to Brailsford and Murray she said, "One policeman after knocking me about for a considerable time, finally took hold of me with his great strong hands like iron just over my heart ... I knew that unless I made a strong effort ... he would kill me."

Although Brailsford and Murray couldn't find a direct link between Black Friday and the death of Mary Clarke, they thought that they had enough evidence to link Henria Williams's death to the way she was treated as part of the deputation that day.

Jessie Murray and Henry Brailsford used the offices of the WSPU in Clement's Inn to interview the women. They thought the witnesses would feel more comfortable in familiar surroundings whilst relating difficult and, for some, embarrassing and humiliating experiences.

On a cold morning in January, the next witness to be called was Rosa Billingham, the woman who was known as the 'cripple suffragette'. Dr Jessie Murray led the questioning of Miss Billingham after introducing Henry.

She said, "Hello Miss Billingham, thank you for agreeing to give us a statement. Can you tell us about what happened to you on Friday the eighteenth of November last year?"

Rosa Billingham replied, "I am lame and cannot walk or get about at all without the aid of my tricycle, and therefore, was obliged to go to the deputation on the machine. At first, the police threw me out of the machine onto the ground in a very brutal manner ... I may also add that my arms and back were so badly bruised and strained by the rough treatment of the police that for two days after Friday 18th I could not leave my bed."

As Miss Billingham was telling her story to Jessie, Henry was taking verbatim notes in shorthand. When she stopped speaking, he looked up and saw that her face was troubled. He said, "I'm sorry that you were treated so harshly and so callously Miss Billingham and I would like to commend you on your fortitude in coming here today and giving evidence."

"Oh but that's not all Mr. Brailsford." She looked at Dr Murray and took a deep breath, then told them the part where the policeman had wheeled her down an alley into a crowd of men and had taken the rivets from her tricycle so that she couldn't escape what lay in store for her.

"What happened then Miss Billingham?" asked Jessie Murray, fearful of what her answer might be.

"Luck was on my side, thankfully, and the men that the policeman had told to do what they wanted to me," she shuddered at the memory of the fear she'd felt at that moment, "apparently had no love for the police and they helped me by putting the rivets back on my machine and wheeling me to safety."

"Well done them!" Brailsford exclaimed.

"Yes," agreed Miss Billingham, smiling for the first time since entering the office, "I then asked them to help a woman who was beaten on the side of the head with a police truncheon, but I don't know what happened to her or how badly hurt she was. She had been helping me back into my machine, you see, after that same policeman had tipped me out onto the ground."

"You'll be pleased to know that she made a full recovery, although she did sustain a fractured skull from the blow to her head," said Brailsford, "We interviewed her in December before she went back to Edinburgh."

"Oh I am so glad to hear that, thank you for letting me know," she said, then she shook her head sadly, "such brutality."

THE FULL REPORT of the investigation was submitted to the Home Office in February by the Conciliation Committee with a covering note which read as follows.

"The gravity of the charges which emerge from these statements impels us to lay the evidence before the Home Office, in the belief that it constitutes a prima facie case for a public enquiry."

However, despite calls for a public enquiry, they were rejected by the Home Secretary, Winston Churchill, a decision which spoke volumes to those calling for a government investigation. Churchill's response was to sweep it under the proverbial carpet after all.

28

ROYAL ALBERT HALL

FEBRUARY 1911

E vangeline and Jessie were among the vast audience of women who filled the Albert Hall to capacity. It was their first rally since Black Friday and the members of the Women's Social and Political Union were in expectant mood, as the wait for the eagerly antici-pated new campaign strategy was about to end.

Mrs Pankhurst was on the stage, alongside her daugh-ters Christabel and Sylvia, and Flora "The General" Drum-mond. Tickets for the venue had sold out days earlier and many people were turned away at the door. Two hundred women stewards, dressed in white, directed the attendees to their seats.

"How do you feel about being back in London?" Evange-line asked Jessie, who was on her first trip away from Edin-burgh since her injuries on "Black Friday" the previous November. They were waiting for Mrs Pankhurst to start the proceedings.

"Ah'm jist fine Evie and, to be honest, Ah'm really excited tae find oot what form the new campaign will take," she replied, her eyes sparkling. Her ordeal had not dampened her enthusiasm for the cause, if anything it had deepened her commitment. She added, "Ah jist love listening tae Mrs Pankhurst speaking, she is so inspiring, is she no'?"

Silence fell as Mrs Pankhurst got to her feet and walked to the front of the stage. Every eye in the hall was on her and you could have heard a pin drop.

She began, "Welcome ladies! Thank you all for coming here today. It is good to see such a wonderful turnout and to those of you who were injured in Parliament Square on the eighteenth of November last, I sincerely hope that you have made a full recovery." There was applause from the audience, then Mrs Pankhurst said, "Before I begin my speech I would ask you to observe a minute's silence in memory of Henria Williams and Mary Clarke who died as a result of their treatment on Black Friday." Every woman in the hall bowed their heads, each with her own thoughts of that truly awful day.

When the tribute had been paid Mrs Pankhurst continued, "We all know the Home Secretary, Mr Churchill, has refused to open a public enquiry into the brutality and excessive violence by the police, against us. The message this sends out is loud and clear: that the government cares more about property than women's lives, therefore I propose that we step up our campaign of attacks on property, particularly the property belonging to members of the Liberal Government and Liberal Members of Parliament." There were loud cheers and calls of "Hear! Hear!" from the audience.

"There will be a relentless smashing of windows, especially those of government buildings and you will receive instructions regarding this from your WSPU branch offices. Unlike our militant activities up until now, where arrest and imprisonment was our aim to gain publicity, you are to avoid being arrested in order to be able to continue to wreak havoc in this war of attrition against this anti-suffrage government." More cheering.

"Finally, 1911 is Census year, when the ten-yearly accounting by government of the country's population is held. Householders are asked to fill in forms giving information on everyone resident, in every property in the country.

This year the Census is to be conducted on the evening of Sunday the second of April and the WSPU, along with the Women's Freedom League, the Actresses Franchise League and many others, will protest by boycotting the Census. Since women apparently don't count as people in the government's eyes, we shall refuse to be counted. Even if you are not a householder, the head of your household - usually or mainly men - will try to add your details on the census form. It is the responsibility of each and every one of you to ensure that your name does not appear on the form. There is ample time to be creative about this ladies, and, no doubt members will share their ideas for achieving this goal. Our slogan is 'No vote, no census!'

Following on from the brutality of the police last year, I have been giving serious consideration as to how we can protect ourselves in this kind of situation. I have been in contact withWilliam and Edith Garrud who are instructors in the martial art of Jiu Jitsu. Our organisation is offering instruction in this art of self defence to all those who wish to avail themselves of it. I'm told that you don't have to be large or particularly strong to use this effectively against big, burly brutes and, in fact, Edith is only four feet, eleven inches. The method uses the brute force of the attacker against them. Classes will begin in London shortly and information will be sent out to all branch offices in due course. Please avail yourselves of this opportunity."

The members of the audience had become very excited by the idea of defending themselves against the police and were chattering away noisily to each other when Mrs Pankhurst spoke again.

"That only leaves me to thank you all for your attendance. Go forth and wreak havoc!"

Every woman in the hall was on her feet clapping and cheering as Mrs Pankhurst and her guests left the stage.

Jessie turned to Evangeline and said, "Oh Evie, Ah cannae wait tae get hame and start planning this next stage in the campaign."

"We don't have to wait until we get home Jess," Evangeline replied, "as long as we have a compartment to ourselves, we'll start planning on the train journey home. Let's get something to eat, I'm famished. All this excitement has given me a voracious appetite."

"Fine wi' me," replied Jessie, "Ah'm that hungry Ah could eat a scabby horse." She chuckled at the sight of Evangeline wrinkling her nose in disgust, then added, "Sorry Evie, that's ma uncouth upbringin', we used tae say that as bairns."

"Well Jess, just for that we're going to the Gardenia Restaurant where you'll have no chance of eating a horse, scabby or otherwise." Evangeline informed her.

"Why's that then Evie?" Jessie asked.

"Because it's a vegetarian restaurant. Many of the suffragettes are vegetarian, some are even vegan."

"What's that when it's at hame?" asked Jessie.

"Come on, I'll explain on the way."

29

THE WSPU OFFICE IN EDINBURGH
EARLY MARCH 1911

E arly in March Evangeline was chairing a meeting in the Edinburgh branch office and the item at the top of the agenda was the 1911 Census and how to avoid being counted.

"Well, I for one, am going to make sure that I am not in either my parents or my grandmother's house on the night of the second of April," announced Evangeline, "although, at this point in time, I haven't a clue as to where I will be so as not to be counted. Does anyone have any suggestions?" She looked around the table at Jessie, Jean, Meg and Mary.

Jessie was thoughtful for a few moments and then said, excitedly, "Why don't we have a party on top of Arthur's Seat? We can build a fire and cook food, bring warm blankets and wear warm clothing and we could even spend the night there. That way none of us will be within a household so we can't be counted." She looked pleased with herself. "What do you think?"

The others smiled and Evangeline said, "Excellent idea Jessie, we'll invite the Edinburgh membership and each woman will be responsible for providing her own food and bedding."

"Ah'm no' sure if Ah'll be able to stay oot a' night," said Meg, sounding disappointed, "Ah have ma mother tae look efter."

"Can't one of your brothers or sisters-in-law stay with her Meg?" asked Jean.

"They're sticklers for obeying the law and if they're meant tae be in their ain hooses, then that's where they'll be," Meg replied, sounding hopeless.

"I've been looking into it," said Evangeline, "and they don't have to be in their own homes as long as they're counted in the property where they are on the night of of the second of April, which would be keeping within their legal obligation for the purpose of the Census."

"Well, Ah could try an' tell them that," Meg replied, not sounding convinced that she would be able to persuade them.

"Can ye no' tell them that ye'll be away on WSPU business?" asked Jean, "they'll maybe think ye're goin' tae London, as ye've done before an' it'll no' be a lie since it is suffragette business, only it'll be Arthur's Seat an' no' Palryment Square," she smiled, pleased to have found a solution for her friend.

"Is yer mother the legal householder, or is it you Meg?" asked Jessie.

"Ma mother is, it's her name on the rent book, although it's me that pays the rent."

"An' will yer Ma fill in the Census form hersel'?" asked Jean.

"Naw, Ah'll have tae dae it for her," said Meg.

"Alright Meg, now this is what you've to do," said Evangeline, "you will write your mother's name only, just before you leave for Arthur's Seat on the night, if you're not there, you can't be counted."

SUCH CENSUS EVASION plans were being made up and down the country. In Dundee ten women stayed overnight in the Dundee office of the WSPU. When the enumerator tried to get in, he found that the door was locked and the front of the building had a poster across it with "No votes, no census" and a banner with their colours was flying from an upper window. The women were not accounted for anywhere else, so they successfully boycotted the 1911 Census.

In the west of the city, at her home in the Perth Road, Ethel Moorhead was giving the enumerator a difficult time when he called. Earlier, when the census form had been delivered, a maid had answered the door and had told him that Ethel's father was the head of the household and so his name was on the form as "head of the house". Having been told this was not the case, he arrived with a new form on the actual night of the census and was shown into a room where her father agreed to supply the required information. When Ethel discovered this she left the room and returned immediately with a large brass bell which she rang every time her father was asked a question, making it extremely difficult for the man to hear what her father was saying. She is reported to have said, "I demand that you leave *my* house now sir." When her father continued to give the man information, she grabbed the form from him and threw it in the fire.

Edinburgh, 2nd April 1911

THIRTY MEMBERS of the Edinburgh branch gathered on the top of Arthur's Seat along with twenty men from the Men's League for Women's Suffrage who were also boycotting the census, but they were also there as a male presence in case of assault or attack from any quarters. The venue was a closely guarded secret, as was their method of boycott, so it was unlikely they would be disturbed, however, they didn't want to take any risks. They had all arrived in little groups on foot and by hackney cab since a large group travelling altogether would draw attention.

Just as twilight was falling. and before settling themselves for the overnight stay, they'd stood and watched the last of the sun going down in the west. A large bonfire had been set in a dip of the hill and by nine o'clock it was blazing well, providing both warmth and cooking facilities.

Evangeline, Jessie, Meg and Jean sat on the edge of the bonfire eating sausages and toasting bread. Several of their members had, like their counterparts in Dundee, decided to spend the night in the Drummond Street office and kept to the back of the premises, so as not to arouse police suspicion by having lights showing at the front.

Evangeline had brought along a couple of bottles of champagne that her grandmother had given her earlier that day. Evangeline smiled as she remembered the old lady's words, "Take these and celebrate Evangeline," she'd said, "and if I was younger I would be joining you," and she had giggled like a schoolgirl and added, "but don't tell your father I said so."

When she had poured the champagne, the four friends raised their glasses in a toast, "To the successful boycott of the 1911 Census!"

To which Evangeline added, "And here's to my generous grandmother!"

"Hear! Hear!" chorused the others.

By midnight the various groups closed around the bonfire for warmth and settled down for the night.

30

8 LAUDER ROAD

MAY 1911

E vangeline was sitting in her grandmother's drawing room on one of her rare evenings at home and she brought up the subject of the Women's Coronation Procession, which was to take place the following month.

"Please say you'll come Grammie, there is going to be a huge contingent from the National Union of Women's Suffrage Societies," she pleaded as she rubbed the ears of the family's lurcher, Rosie, who was in her usual place on the sofa.

"Oh, I don't think so Evangeline," replied the older woman, "I think I'm getting a bit old for processions, besides it's a long journey to London and who would look after Rosie?"

At the sound of her name, Rosie raised her head and looked at her mistress, ears out expectantly. When the hoped-for tasty morsel didn't materialise, she put her head back on Evangeline's lap.

"Betty would look after Rosie, of course, and you're not too old for a trip to London," Evangeline said, spiritedly.

"We can all stay in Father's flat near Westminster, it's large enough with four bedrooms, you'd be very comfortable, you know."

"I do know how big the London flat is my dear," she said with a twinkle in her eyes, "your Mother and I have stayed there a few times when we were on shopping trips."

"That's the other thing Grammie," she informed her grandmother, "gThe Women's Social and Political Union might be organising it, but all the suffrage organisations in the country have been invited to take part. As I said earlier, the NUWSS will be there, along with the Women's Freedom League, the Actresses Franchise League and many, many others." Her words were falling over each other in her excitement and enthusiasm, "Do you know that women are coming from all parts of the Empire and other parts of the world too?"

Charlotte, who was beginning to catch some of her granddaughter's enthusiasm said, "You make it sound so exciting and such a special occasion Evangeline, that it would be a pity to miss it. I'll talk to Letty and Louisa tomorrow, we would all enjoy the trip. Perhaps your grandmother Moncrieff would like to join us too."

"It's going to be the spectacle of the century Grammie," she said, with great enthusiasm, " and it will certainly outdo the all-male boring coronation procession for the King the following week."

"Tut, tut," said her grandmother, "that's not very respectful and it's not what the Women's Coronation Procession is for."

"Oh but it is, Grammie, it's exactly what it's for, that and other reasons," she said with a stubborn lift of her chin.

"I don't think I understand dear," said her grandmother,

a little confused, "I thought it was to celebrate King George V's coronation."

"Ostensibly it is, but it's *the* perfect opportunity to make we women visible, to demonstrate that, we too, that is half the population of this country, mind you Grandmother," she only called her *grandmother* when she was on her 'high horse', "that we too are the King's loyal subjects. The half of the population that doesn't have the right to vote."

"Yes, I see what you mean, dear and I have to agree with you when you put it like that," replied a thoughtful Charlotte.

"There are going to be famous women from over the centuries depicted, those who have contributed to the world: scientists, such as Marie Curie, martyrs like Joan of Arc, authors and past queens, including Boudica and Mary Queen of Scots and her cousin Elizabeth." She was thoughtful for a few moments then said, "I don't understand why Queen Victoria was so against the female franchise Grammie, do you?"

"No Evangeline, I don't," replied Charlotte, "perhaps because she had no need of it, who knows?"

"Once you have confirmation that Mother, Aunt Letty and Grandmama Moncrieff will attend, let me know and I'll make all the necessary travel arrangements," said Evangeline. "It will be easier that way rather than everyone booking their own tickets and this way we shall all be seated together on the train."

"I shall let you know as soon as I have spoken to the others Evangeline," replied her grandmother, will Jessie be one of our party?" Charlotte was aware of her granddaughter's close relationship with the, still married, woman, even though she was estranged from her husband. She had surprised herself by being quite accepting of the arrangement since Evangeline had been a much happier young woman since becoming close with Jessie Gilhooley.

"Yes, of course, Grammie," replied Evangeline, smiling, "I wouldn't go anywhere without Jessie, she's my second in command."

Charlotte smiled fondly at Evangeline and said, "Well I think I'll retire now, I'm feeling rather tired with all this talk of processions and travel to London. Goodnight my dear, and thank you for inviting me to such a special event." She stood up and kissed Evangeline on the cheek, then said, "Come along Rosie, it's time for your last ablutions before we go upstairs to bed." Ever since Henry had died Rosie had taken her place in her mistress's bedroom as her protector. She sometimes slept at the foot of the big four-poster bed, but she also had a comfortable, cosy dog bed by the fireside. Charlotte believed in Rosie having a choice.

Downstairs, Evangeline sat on, with a paper and pencil, making notes of the arrangements she would need to have in place for the female contingent of the Frobisher family's upcoming trip to London for the Women's Coronation Procession.

31

LONDON

17TH JUNE 1911

T he Edinburgh contingent of the Women's Social and Political Union were together in line, and Evangeline and Jessie were holding their banner high. Evangeline's grandmother, mother and Aunt Letty were further back with the Scottish branches of the National Union of Women's Suffrage Societies.

There was a buzz of excitement which went all the way back to where more and more groups were joining the lengthy queue of women standing five abreast holding the banners of their particular organisations. Forty thousand women were taking part and thousands of people thronged the streets, waiting with excited anticipation for the procession to begin.

"Oh look Evie," said Jessie, "here comes The General tae start the proceedins."

The "General", Flora Drummond, was on horseback and she was to lead the procession. At five-thirty sharp she slowly led the the WSPU, followed by all the other suffrage organisations, including the NUWSS, the largest of all the participating groups. Louisa's mother, Lady Moncrieff had decided not to go as she was having a painful arthritic episode and she would not have been able to walk very far, or sit for a long period on the train.

Before Louisa left, she had said, "Louisa, I want you to be my eyes and ears and when you return you must tell me all about it and I shall experience it vicariously."

"Of course I will Mother," Louisa had replied, "I'm just so sorry you won't be there."

Now Letty and Louisa were walking on either side of Charlotte and they were all transfixed by the sheer number of women with their creative and colourful banners. They marvelled at the floats, especially the exotic one which depicted the new King's Empire, and the "Historical pageant of Great Women" that Evangeline had so excitedly told her grandmother about. There were women dressed in their native Welsh and Irish costumes as well as a small group of Indian women.

The mood of both those marching and those spectating was vibrant and celebratory and they were accompanied by music as the procession wound its way through the city's streets for almost seven miles. Several hundred women and girls were dressed to represent the suffragette prisoners.

It was generally agreed that the Women's Coronation Procession was a resounding success and the logistical planning for such a large number of people had been meticulously organised and executed with precision-timing, just like that of the King's Coronation which was due to take place five days later.

AFTERWARDS, back in Charles's flat, the five women were tired but exhilarated and they were discussing the events of the evening over tea and sandwiches which Louisa had prepared earlier and had covered with a damp tea towel so they wouldn't dry out.

"What an absolutely fabulous turnout!" exclaimed Letty, "and to think I nearly missed it. Thank goodness Wilf persuaded me that I wouldn't be needed at the practice, I really wouldn't have missed it for the world." She sighed with pleasure.

"You'll have to come with me when I tell Mother all about it," Louisa said to her mother-in-law, "in case I leave anything out. I promised her I would take it all in and report back."

"Don't worry dear," replied Charlotte, "it will be my pleasure. In fact. I'll be telling everyone I meet about it, whether they want to hear it or not," she laughed, looking much younger than her eighty-two years.

Evangeline smiled, as she and Jessie listened to the three older women talking so enthusiastically. Only she and Jessie knew just how fragile an alliance it had been between the WSPU who had organised the event, and the other organisations who advocated more constitutional means of campaigning to get the vote, and who disapproved of the suffragettes militant, and often violent, methods. They believed that the militants were actually harming the cause of women's suffrage rather than taking it forward.

"Let's hope that such a show will convince those in power, as well as those who say that it is only a small number of women in the population who want the vote, that we are serious about it." said Evangeline, "I say actions speak louder than words," she raised her teacup, "A toast to each and every woman there today, well done!"

The others raised their teacups too and chorused, "Well done!"

Louisa yawned and said, "I don't know about anyone

else, but I'm tired and shall go to bed now. I want to be fresh for our shopping trip tomorrow."

"Me too," replied Letty.

"I'll join you," said Charlotte and they all got up. They said goodnight to Evangeline and Jessie and went off to their bedrooms.

Evangeline and Jessie sat on for a while, talking in low tones about the Women's Coronation Procession.

32

WEDNESDAY 3RD APRIL 1912, 7.30PM

T he Conciliation Bills of 1911 and 1912 also failed to
be passed by Parliament, with the opportunity for
one million women being granted the right to vote
being defeated by only fourteen votes. On the 29th of March
1912 two hundred and eight Members of Parliament voted
for giving propertied women the vote, with two hundred
and twenty-two voting against it.

After ceasing militant activity whilst the Bill made its
way through the parliamentary process, the suffragettes
once again resumed their activities with a sustained window
smashing campaign.

The campaign, in the wake of the three times defeated
Conciliation Bill, was being systematically carried out by
suffragettes throughout the length and breadth of the
United Kingdom.

Thirty women were gathered in the meeting room of the
WSPU Edinburgh branch office and the excitement was
palpable. Evangeline Frobisher was chairing the meeting.

"Alright ladies, you will be divided into three groups,"
she said, looking around the table. Some of the women were

standing since this was an 'extra-ordinary meeting' of the Edinburgh members and there wasn't enough seating for everyone. She had considered hiring a hall but this mission had to be of the utmost secrecy if it was to work and she couldn't risk the police becoming aware of what they had planned.

She continued, "You have all been allocated your areas. I will be in charge of the Princes Street group, Meg is over-seeing the George Street group and Jessie is leading the women who will be in the High Street, you will have to act with speed there, of course," she said, addressing Jessie, "because of the proximity to the High Street police station and you will most likely be the first ones to be arrested."

"We've been over the plan," Jessie replied, "and we'll start wi' the Bank o' Scotland Head Office at the top o' Bank Street an' then cut up behind the High Court and go on fae there."

"Excellent!" said Evangeline, nodding her approval.

She then looked at the clock on the wall and said, "At eight-thirty, precisely, you will be in your positions, ready to smash as many windows as possible, before you are appre-hended. Avoid arrest if you can, Mrs Pankhurst wants as many of us as possible to be at liberty to continue and esca-late this campaign. Once you're satisfied that you have done sufficient damage, move on to the next one," she instructed. "Now, do you all have your tools?"

The women all drew out little hammers from their muffs or bags and Jessie's group also had stones to throw at the windows out of reach in the High Street buildings. Suffragettes up and down the country had been receiving instructions from their male friends in the skill of throwing stones and hitting targets and they were now all confident and proficient with stones and targets.

"Excellent!" Evangeline said again. "Jessie, since your group is travelling to the your target by foot, I would suggest that you spread yourselves out, walking in two's and three's. Ten of you altogether would certainly arouse suspicion."

"Nae worries Evangeline," replied Jessie.

"Meg," she turned to look at her, "Our groups will have to travel on the same tram to Princes Street," then turning to the others around the table, she added, "like Jessie's group we'll arrange ourselves as though we are separate groups of women on our way into town for the evening."

"A'right Evangeline," replied Meg, "we could even spread ourselves between two tram stops tae be less conspicuous."

"Good thinking," Evangeline said and she stood up. "Let's get ready to go ladies, do your best and good luck; at least the weather is favourable this evening," she added, looking out of the window. "We'll meet back here later this evening, that is, those of us who are still free to do so, to assess the success or otherwise, of tonight's activities and we shall plan our next operation."

They all got up and put on their coats and hats, chattering excitedly, looking forward to paying the Liberal Government for failing to secure the passage of the Conciliation Bill for the third year in a row.

Evangeline, in particular, was looking forward to the evening's activities with enthusiasm and relish, and she smiled to herself as she left.

33

A SHORT TIME LATER

Princes Street

E vangeline alighted from the tram at the east end of Princes Street, at the top of the Waverley Steps, along with three other women. The other two groups of three, would get off in the middle and west end, respectively.

There were only a few people on the street, although the road was busy with motor cars, hackney cabs and trams. The plan was that Evangeline's women would work from Register House to Jenners, just opposite the Scott Monument, with the others taking from there to Frederick Street and the last section was starting at the West End and working back from there. Jenners and Maule's Department Stores were the prime targets and to be worked on first, in case of arrest.

Evangeline waited for a break in the traffic then she said, "Let's go ladies, we have a lot to accomplish tonight!" and all four crossed the street quickly and walked towards Jenners at a brisk pace.

Jenners was an upmarket store, patronised by Edinburgh's wealthy citizens. It was a big store with large window displays running along Princes Street, around the corner and up as far as Rose Street.

When they reached the store Evangeline said, "Alright ladies, spread yourselves along the length of the windows and do as much damage as possible."

At first it seemed that her small hammer was making little impact, but Evangeline persevered until suddenly a long crack appeared and the window shattered with fragments of broken glass raining over the display of fur coats and other items of Ladies' fashion.

She then hurried around the corner where there was a display of men's clothing, top hats and walking sticks. "Right then," she said to the empty street, "this is for every woman who was force-fed," and now that she had the hang of it, she found it easier to break the glass. Before long, showers of broken glass were covering the display of mannequins, clothes and everything else in the window.

Just as she was standing back to admire her work, Mary and Wilma came running around the corner.

"Run Evangeline!" Mary shouted, "a cab driver stopped his motor, got out and grabbed Elsie and he's sent his passenger to fetch the police."

All three ran up the street and around St Andrew's Square, as previously arranged, where they slowed to a walk, then returned to Princes Street to catch the tram back to Drummond Street.

The Old Town

MEANWHILE, Jessie's group had been busy in the Old Town. After Jessie and three of her group had broken several of the Bank of Scotland's windows, at the top of the Mound, they hurried up Bank Street to the front of the High Court where Jessie proceeded to break the small window panes on the ground floor. She was just about to use the remaining stones on the windows of the upper floor when she heard the sharp blast of a police whistle.

As previously agreed, on hearing that the police were aware of their activities, they were to make their way, individually, back to Drummond Street as quickly and as inconspicuously as possible. Jessie hurried across the High Street and slipped, unseen, around the corner into George IV Bridge.

The other three, who were breaking windows of the Court of Session and the Signet Library across in Parliament Square, ceased operations and tried to make their escape. Unfortunately, two of the three found themselves trapped in Parliament Square with no means of getting away as four large policemen rushed towards them and roughly grabbed hold of them by the arms. Each were thinking the same thing: that it was a pity that there were two constables to each woman, otherwise they could have used their skill in Jiu Jitsu to disable the big men and escape being caught, as they had on previous occasions.

They were marched down to the police station at 192 High Street, charged with malicious damage and kept in the cells overnight, before appearing at the Sheriff Court next morning.

The remaining three women from Jessie's group managed to smash twenty panes of glass in the ground floor windows of the City Chambers before a night watchman came out to see what the commotion was. He blew a whistle to summon any constables that might be in the vicinity, but the women, dressed from head to toe in black, slipped away quickly down the steps of Cockburn Street and up Waverley Bridge to the tram stop in Princes Street.

George Street

MEG'S GROUP succeeded in smashing several shop and bank windows in George Street and at the first sound of a police whistle, they hurried down Frederick Street and along Rose Street, always quiet at this time of night, to Princes Street and then back to the office by tram.

By ten o'clock, twenty-five of the thirty women who had set out on the window breaking spree were seated around the meeting room table and were all talking excitedly when Evangeline called the meeting to order.

"May I congratulate you ladies on evading arrest by the police." She did a quick head count then said, "Will the group leaders tell us how your mission went and how many women you lost into police custody. Jessie, you go first."

Jessie said, "Two o' ma lot, Emily and Victoria, havenae returned, so we can safely assume that they're in the polis cells in the High Street. We'll go tae the Sheriff Court in the mornin' and support them at their trial."

"And the damage?" asked Evangeline.

"We smashed a good lot o' windaes in the bank, the High Court and the City Chambers, but it wis a close thing, and thank heavens for the polis's loud whistles gie'en us warnin' that they were on their way." She chuckled and added, "Ah wonder if they realise what a big help that is." The others around the table laughed too.

"How did your group fare?" Evangeline looked at Meg.

"We managed tae smash several plate glass windaes in the posh gent's outfitters, opposite the Assembly Rooms, an' the windaes o' three banks, along the length o' George Street, are well an' truly broken," Meg replied. "There'll be some drafts blowin' in there the morn's mornin'. We were lucky tae have only one arrested, but then George Street is quiet at night wi' little traffic until the Assembly Rooms empty later on."

"Excellent!" replied Evangeline, "so you all live to fight another day. I lost two from my group. Elsie was accosted by a passing cab driver while his passenger fetched a constable," she told the others, "and Elizabeth escaped arrest by jumping onto a passing tram at the West End, when four constables who, incidentally didn't blow their whistles, crept up on the women and blocked any escape route."

"Quick thinking Elizabeth," said Jessie, in admiration.

"No' really Jessie," replied Elizabeth honestly, "it wis mair like good timin' oan the part o' the tram driver," she smiled, self-deprecatingly.

"So," said Evangeline, "we have five women appearing in court tomorrow. As many of us as possible must be there in solidarity with them," although she knew some of them had to be at work and couldn't afford to lose a few hours pay, even to support their suffragette sisters.

She concluded the meeting by saying, "It's time to go home ladies. I hope you have a peaceful night's sleep, see you at the Sheriff Court tomorrow. Goodnight."

Jessie stayed behind with Evangeline while the others collected their things and left the office, calling their "goodnights" to each other.

Once the front door had been closed and locked, Evangeline and Jessie hugged each other for a long moment, then Jessie said, "Oh Evie, Ah wis that glad tae see ye when

Ah got back here, Ah couldnae have tholed it if ye'd been arrested an' sent tae the Calton Gaol."

Evangeline smiled and placed a lingering kiss on Jessie's lips, then said "I am too Jess, and I was so relieved to see you coming through the door. Let's go upstairs. But first I'll telephone Grammie and let her know I'm staying here tonight, I don't want her worrying. She seemed to know we had something going on tonight, although I didn't mention anything to her."

"Maybe she has the "sixth sense", as ma Irish granny used tae say," replied Jessie, smiling. She was glad Evangeline was going to stay the night and they could fall asleep in each other's arms. "Ah'll away up and light the gas fire."

Much later, after making love tenderly, they both fell into a dreamless, restful sleep.

34

4 HATTON PLACE

THURSDAY 4TH APRIL 1912

L ouisa was in the drawing room reading when Charles burst into the room, flourishing that afternoon's edition of the *Edinburgh Evening News*. Charles was home for the Easter recess and had been coming back from his constituency office when he saw the newspaper headlines on the news stand. "This is the last straw!" he growled.

Louisa looked up, startled, and asked, "What's the matter Charles?"

"Evangeline has to be responsible for this," he said, stabbing the paper with his index finger. "Listen to this!"

Sitting on the armchair opposite Louisa, he read the article to her.

"WINDOWS ALL OVER EDINBURGH SMASHED TO SMITHEREENS, SUFFRAGETTES CAUGHT RED-HANDED!

Last night, in simultaneous attacks, the windows of prominent properties, in both the Old and New Town, were broken in what can only be described as a spree of vandalism.

In the Old Town the windows of the Head Office of the Bank of Scotland, at the top of the Mound, had its ground floor windows broken, to the extent that whole windows need to be replaced.

The windows of the High Court were also damaged, as were some in the City Chambers where the night watchman, Wullie Dougan, interrupted women, dressed in dark clothes, breaking ground floor windows. He blew his whistle to summon the police, but the culprits escaped down the steps of Fleshmarket Close leading to Cockburn Street.

Fortunately police arrested two women before they could do much damage to to the Signet Library in Parliament Square.

In the New Town, a great deal of damage was done to the large plate glass windows of shops in Princes Street and George Street, with Jenners and Maule's Department Stores receiving the worst of the damage with fragments of glass ruining some display items.

Three banks, the British Linen, the Clydesdale and the Royal Bank of Scotland, all in George Street, were also victims of this malicious mischief.

It is not known how many women were involved in this, obviously premeditated, attack but five women were arrested at the various scenes, all members of the Women's Social and Political Union, and they came before the Sheriff Court this morning.

They were named as Elsie Nugent, Emily Bryce, Victoria MacKinnon, Mary Wilson and Bernadette Flynn. Handing down their sentences, Sheriff Michael Mathison said,

"You were all caught in the act of committing malicious

damage to property for which you will each pay a fine of twenty pounds or serve three months in prison." There were gasps of shock from the women's supporters in the public gallery when the substantial sum of twenty pounds was mentioned, an amount that even the wealthy would balk at, and there was no way these women could raise such a sum. The sheriff went on, "I must warn you that such acts will not further your cause and will only serve to turn the public against you."

This produced shouts of "Shame on you!" and "Votes for Women" from the supporters in the courtroom.

"Silence!" shouted the sheriff, banging his gavel, "or you will be held in contempt of court and imprisoned without the option."

The courtroom fell silent and the sheriff asked the women if they were prepared to pay the fines or be sent to prison. It is believed that he had deliberately set the fines high in the hope they would not have the funds to pay them, in which case the five women would be off the streets for some time.

They all opted for imprisonment and were removed to the court cells to await transportation to the Calton Gaol."

LOUISA HAD BEEN LISTENING with bated breath when Charles got to the part about the arrests, then heaved a sigh of relief when Evangeline's name wasn't mentioned.

"Oh Charles, it's just getting worse and worse," said Louisa wringing her hands and shaking her head, "I can't bear to think of what they're going to do next."

"If only more members had voted for the Conciliation Bill, then none of this senseless damage would be happening and we could be getting on with our lives and the job of governing the country," said Charles, heatedly. "I don't know which is making me more angry, Louisa, those stubborn MP's or the WSPU."

"At least Evangeline wasn't arrested," said Louisa, looking on the bright side.

"This time ..." replied Charles.

"But I do fear for those poor women who will go on hunger strike and be forcibly fed."

"I'll just call Mother," said Charles, "see if she knows anything, you never know, Evangeline may have confided in her. Those two have become extremely close since she moved in with Mother."

When Charles returned to the drawing room he was frowning and Louisa asked, "Is there anything wrong Charles?"

"No, not really. She didn't go home last night but she telephoned Mother to let her know. She stayed in the flat above the office with Jessie."

"Well that's alright, isn't it Charles?" replied Louisa.

"I hope so," he said, shaking his head, "I don't know Louisa, I just get the feeling that Evangeline and Jessie are very close, more than just friends."

Louisa looked surprised and asked, "Do you mean that you think they're lovers Charles? No, that's ridiculous, they're just very good friends."

"Is it ridiculous Louisa? After all, Evangeline has never had any young beaus, has she? Not one romantic relationship and she's twenty-five," he said.

"That's because she's so busy with her suffrage work, she doesn't have time for romance," replied Louisa. "Wait until we get the vote, that will all change then."

Charles looked at her and smiled, "I'm sure you're right

my dear." But what he was thinking was that Louisa could be very child-like in her naivety at times.

"Let's have a sherry before supper," she said, "and you can tell me about your day at the constituency office. Let's forget all about broken windows and acts of militancy for now."

"Excellent idea, Louisa," he said and went over to the sideboard to pour them both a glass of sherry.

35

ESCALATION OF MILITANCY

1912-1913

The loyal members of the Women's Social and Political Union dedicated themselves even more to the cause after the third Conciliation Bill's failure to become law. There was much frustration following this and Evangeline and Jessie attended a speech given by Mrs Pankhurst in The Royal Albert Hall on the seventeenth of October in 1912. They sat, enthralled by her words.

"There is a great deal of criticism of this movement ladies and gentlemen, criticism from gentlemen who do not hesitate to order out armies to slay and kill their opponents, who do not hesitate to encourage party mobs who attack defenceless women when they attend public meetings. Criticism from them hardly rings true." "Hear! Hear!" Evangeline called out before she could stop herself. She knew, from personal experience, that there had been many occasions when suffragettes were attacked by mobs of men and Mrs Pankhurst herself was once knocked to the ground, unconscious, from a blow by a man.

Mrs Pankhurst continued. "I get letters from ladies who claim to be ardent suffragists who implore me to urge the members not to be reckless with human lives. The only recklessness suffragists have shown about human lives has been about their own lives and not about the lives of others and I say here and now that it never has been and never will be the policy of the Women's Social and Political Union to endanger human life." There was a burst of applause from the audience then Mrs Pankhurst held up her hand for silence.

She went on, "We leave that to the enemy, we leave that to the men and their warfare. It is not the method of women. No, even from the point of view of public policy, militancy affecting the security of human life would be out of place.

There is something the governments care for more than human life and that is the security of property and so it is through property that we shall strike the enemy." There were more cheers and calls of "Well said!" and "Hear! Hear!".

Evangeline and Jessie were holding hands and Evangeline squeezed Jessie's hand in a show of their solidarity with Mrs Pankhurst.

She spoke more insistently now. "Be militant, each in your own way. Those of you who can, express your militancy by going to the House of Commons and refusing to leave without satisfaction, as we did in the early days, do so.

Those of you who can express your militancy by facing Party mobs at Cabinet Ministers' meetings when you remind them of their falseness to principle, do so.

Those of you who can express your militancy by joining us in our anti-government by-election policy, do so." The Women's Social and Political Union had long since targeted Liberal candidates standing in by-elections and supporting their opponents, with some degree of success. Even if a

Liberal candidate won, it was often with a reduced majority.

"Those of you who can break windows, break them. Those of you who can still further attack the sacred idol of property, so as to make the Government realise that property is as greatly endangered by women's suffrage as it was by the Chartists of old, do so.

And my last word is to the Government, I incite this meeting to rebellion!"

Every member of the audience got to their feet and applauded. Evangeline and Jessie hugged each other and Jessie shouted, above the clamour in the hall, "Ah cannae wait tae get hame Evie, tae continue wi' our rebellion."

After the escalation of militant acts that followed this speech, the Trustees of the Royal Albert Hall banned Mrs Pankhurst, her daughters and the WSPU from further use of it.

Between 1912 and 1913, up and down the length of the country, pillar boxes were set alight, bombs were planted in, or near, the homes of government ministers. The most infamous example was when two bombs were planted in the house of the Chancellor, David Lloyd George by Emily Wilding Davison, but only one went off. No one was hurt but there was a lot of damage to the property.

The members of the Women's Social and Political Union had taken Mrs Pankhurst's words to heart and they wreaked havoc in many areas of public life. It was the suffragettes who invented the letter bomb and many exploded in transit; telegraph wires were cut and bombs were planted on train lines and in empty train carriages. The bomb planted outside the Bank of England in Threadneedle Street, was discovered and safely defused.

A plot to blow up the grandstand at Crystal Palace was

foiled on the eve of the 1913 F.A. Cup final, and, in the Scottish Borders four women were arrested whilst trying to set fire to the new stand at Kelso racecourse.

It seemed that no part of the country escaped the escalating attacks on property and the suffragettes were accused of being terrorists.

With the militant acts being carried out on such a large scale, so too did the number of women being arrested increase, followed by imprisonment and hunger striking.

36

ROYAL SCOTTISH ACADEMY, EDINBURGH

THURSDAY 20TH FEBRUARY 1913

At ten o'clock on a cold February morning Evangeline climbed the steps of the art gallery at the foot of the Mound. She was wrapped up in a long warm, red woollen coat with a fur collar and matching fur hat and muff. She looked like any other wealthy patron of the gallery and the doorman bowed as he held the door open for her to enter.

She spent around fifteen minutes, ostensibly looking at the paintings, then she sat down on a bench, in the Great Room, opposite the Lavery portrait of King George V. She waited until a couple, who'd been looking at the KIng's portrait, had left the room then she stood up and walked towards the painting. Looking around, and satisfied that she was alone, she took a small hatchet from inside her muff and proceeded to slash the painting. As she raised her arm for the fourth time, it was caught, mid-swing, by one of the gallery's stewards and the hatchet was wrenched from her hand.

The police were called and she was arrested and brought before the sheriff the following day.

Jessie had known that Evangeline had something planned but she could not persuade her to tell her what it was.

"Evangeline," she'd said to her in the office that morning, "why don't ye tell me what's goin' on?" You've never kept secrets before an' ye've been edgy for days."

Evangeline replied, "I won't tell you Jess because I don't want you coming with me, one of us needs to be free to run the office and plan the campaign."

"So ye're sure ye're gonnae be arrested an' get the gaol then?"

Evangeline didn't meet her gaze, nor did she reply. She simply put on her gloves and kissed Jessie on the cheek and said, "Goodbye Jessie dear, if I'm not back by noon get an *Evening News* this afternoon" and then she left the office.

JESSIE DID as Evangeline instructed and got a late afternoon edition of the newspaper. It was front page headline news.

"KING'S PORTRAIT SLASHED BY SUFFRAGETTE

A young woman, named as Miss Evangeline Frobisher, walked boldly into the Great Room of the Royal Scottish Academy this morning, took a small hatchet from somewhere on her person and proceeded to slash and hack the portrait of King George V which was a recent acquisition by the gallery. She was seized by a gallery steward and the hatchet was taken off her. The police were called and she was arrested. She will appear in the Sheriff Court tomorrow.

The doorman, who had admitted Miss Frobisher when she entered the building, told us, "I'm that shocked Sir, I never would have let her in if I'd known she was one of those suffragettes, but she looked like a lady, if you know what I mean." We will bring you all the latest news from Miss Frobisher's trial as and when we have it."

The first thing Jessie did after reading the paper was to telephone Evangeline's grandmother to let her know about her arrest; she then contacted several WSPU members to make sure they spread the word that support would be needed for Evangeline's appearance in court the following day.

4 Hatton Place, that afternoon.

A SHOCKED AND pale Louisa had just received a telephone call from her mother-in-law to let her know about Evangeline's arrest and why she was arrested. She stood by the telephone for several moments wondering what she should do. She would have to warn Charles but he would be on the train on his way back to Edinburgh. Charles was conscientious about being in his constituency office on Fridays to be available for anyone who needed to see him.

Louisa finally made a decision and went into the kitchen where Maggie was rolling out pastry for the steak and kidney pie they would have for supper that evening.

"Maggie," she said, "I'm sorry for any inconvenience, but we shall want supper an hour later than usual and I'm just going out for a short while."

"Very well Lady Frobisher," replied a cheerful Maggie, "it's no' any inconvenience tae me."

Louisa had been having pains in her legs for some weeks which, at first, were intermittent, but nowadays, seemed to be there all the time, making every step she took painful. She had put it down to the very cold and damp weather they'd had since the new year but she now decided to consult Letty for something to help soothe the pain and, on the way, she would buy a copy of the *Evening News*. She thought it would be helpful to share her worries with her friend.

She went up to her bedroom and picked out her warmest coat and boots from the wardrobe and got ready to go out.

She got into the car, carefully, trying not to wince as she lifted her legs as she sat down in the driving seat. She took several deep breaths then she drove off towards the Salisbury Medical Practice.

On the way she pulled up outside a newsagent in Grange Road and bought a copy of the *Evening News*, then sat in the car while she read the short article. "Oh my God!" she said, "what have you done this time Evangeline? And what is your father going to say? The King's portrait, of all the things you could have chosen to damage!" She drove on to Salisbury Place and parked the car outside the medical practice.

Rose, as usual, was working at the reception desk and her face lit up when she saw Louisa. "Good afternoon Lady Frobisher," she said, "are you here to see Dr Letty? She didn't mention that you would be coming in this afternoon."

"No Rose, she doesn't know," replied Louisa, trying hard to inject some cheerfulness into her voice, "it was a spur of the moment decision. Is she too busy to see me? I don't mind waiting."

"As it happens, you're in luck, her last patient has just left and she's still in her consulting room," Rose told her, "just go along."

Louisa knocked on Letty's door and went in. Letty, who

was writing the notes on her last patient, looked up and smiled when she saw Louisa.

"Hello Louisa," she said, "this is a lovely surprise, is it a social visit?" She frowned as she saw Louisa walking slowly and painfully across the room and then sat down.

"Whatever is the matter Louisa?" she asked, coming around from her desk and sitting down on the chair beside her friend.

Louisa tried to smile as she said, "Actually Letty, it's both social and medical."

Louisa explained about the increasing discomfort and the pain in her legs and Letty told her to lie on the couch while she examined her.

Afterwards, when she was once more sitting in front of Letty's desk, Letty said, "I think it is some kind of arthritic or rheumatic issue Louisa. There is no swelling in your joints and perhaps the cold and damp is aggravating it."

"I was hoping you could give me something to soothe the pain."

"I can certainly do that, and maybe a warm bath in the morning to help soothe the aches before you get moving, might be a good idea too."

Louisa nodded and said, "Thank you Letty, I appreciate your help."

"You said it was a social visit too Louisa."

"Yes, I need to talk to you about something that has just come up Letty," she replied and she put the *Evening News* on the desk where Letty could see the headlines. It didn't take her long to read the short but devastating article.

"Oh Louisa, you must be terribly upset!" she said.

At the kind words from her friend, Louisa could no longer hold back the tears that had been threatening since the telephone call from her mother-in-law. Letty hurried around the desk to comfort her.

When Louisa finally stopped crying, she said, "Charles is coming home this evening and I don't know how I'm going to tell him. I'm meeting him off the train at seven o'clock this evening."

"Do you think he'll have seen the report in a newspaper before he gets to Edinburgh?"

"No, I don't think so, the story will not have reached the south yet, but it's sure to be in all the national and regional newspapers by tomorrow morning," Louisa replied, "Oh Letty, what are we going to do with Evangeline?"

Letty took Louisa's hand in hers and said gently, "I'm afraid there isn't anything you can do Louisa, she's her own woman now and she knows what she's doing. It's all got out of hand since the failure of the third Conciliation Bill and Mrs Pankhurst's 'incitement to rebellion'."

"I know you're right Letty, but I just feel so powerless to do anything."

"Meet Charles off the train and drive him home. Pour him a stiff brandy, tell him something dreadful has happened and give him the paper to read," Letty advised.

Later that day, that is exactly what Louisa did. Charles, as expected, was extremely angry at both what he regarded as wanton destruction of property and the repercussions for his reputation and career as a Liberal politician.

37

EDINBURGH SHERIFF COURT

FRIDAY 21ST FEBRUARY 1913

T he public gallery was filled to capacity with supporters of Evangeline. The trial was being presided over by Sheriff MacConachie and the room fell silent as he entered the court.

The Clerk of the Court bowed to the sheriff and opened the proceedings. "Call Miss Evangeline Frobisher."

Presently, Evangeline was led up the stairs from the cells in the basement, flanked by two constables. As soon as she appeared in the dock, a great cheer went up from her suffragette friends.

The sheriff banged his gavel and called, "Silence!" then the Clerk, after asking for her name and swearing her in said, "Miss Evangeline Frobisher you are charged with a breach of the peace and causing malicious damage to a portrait of His Majesty, King George V, in the Great Room of the Royal Academy on Thursday the twentieth of February How do you plead?"

Evangeline stood up up and looked unrepentant. "I admit legal responsibility for the damage but I am engaged in a political campaign for women's enfranchisement and I therefore hold the government morally responsible," she replied.

There was an uproar in the gallery with shouts of "Well said!" and "Hear! Hear!"

"Silence!" the sheriff called again and added, "If there is one more disruption I shall have the public gallery cleared," then he turned to Evangeline and said, "So, Miss Frobisher, you are pleading guilty."

Evangeline said nothing and the sheriff continued, "You were caught in the act of damaging the King's portrait and are, therefore, guilty of malicious damage. I sentence you to three months imprisonment without the option." and, banging his gavel, he said, "Court dismissed."

Evangeline was then led back down to the cells to be transported to the Calton Gaol to begin her three month prison sentence.

Wednesday 30th April,
Outside the Calton Gaol

JESSIE WAS WAITING outside the prison along with a number of other WSPU women on the morning that Evangeline was released from prison.

As she emerged through the prison door Jessie gasped in shock at the pathetic figure of her friend and lover. She hurried forward and gently embraced Evangeline while the other women clapped and cheered. Jessie's heart sank as she felt Felt Evangeline's ribs and shoulder blades through her clothes.

Evangeline had served just over two months of her sentence when she was released under the Prisoners (Temporary Discharge for Ill-Health) Act 1913, commonly known as the "Cat and Mouse Act".

It was how the Liberal Government tried to solve the problem of hunger-striking suffragettes and ended the need for force-feeding. When a woman's health deteriorated due to being on hunger strike, they were released on a temporary basis and, when their health had recovered sufficiently, they had to return to prison to continue to serve their sentence.

Unfortunately for Evangeline, the Act came into force when she had already served two thirds of her sentence, on the twenty-fifth of April, by which time she had been force-fed more than one hundred times. She had got to the stage where she had no more energy to resist the tube being put up her nose or down her throat and she just lay there and let them do what they would.

"It's so good tae see ye Evie," Jessie said, "Ah'll take ye hame tae Lauder Road and get yer Aunt Letty tae examine ye an' we'll both look efter ye until ye're well again."

Evangeline's voice was barely more than a whisper as she said, "I've still got twenty-two days of my sentence to serve Jessie and, as soon as I'm well enough, I'll be rearrested and sent back to prison."

"Well we'll no' think aboot that jist now Evie," replied Jessie, "look, ye've got a welcomin' committee."

Evangeline looked at the well-known faces of the women who had come out to cheer her and she mouthed a "thank you" to them, smiling, which only served to highlight her hollow cheeks and the, now sharp-looking, cheek bones.

"Ah've got a hackney cab waiting Evie, we'll have ye tucked up in bed in nae time."

Jessie helped her into the waiting vehicle and they drove

off to the cheers from the women who had come to greet her on her first day of freedom.

Awaiting them in Lauder Road were her mother, grand-mother and Aunt Letty and they were all shocked as they watched the frail figure being helped out of the cab by Jessie.

"Now Louisa," said her mother-in-law, "I know it's going to be difficult for you, but please try not to fuss. You know what Evangeline is like when you do that and Letty will look after her so there's no need to worry."

"Yes Mother-in-law," she replied meekly, "I think I've learned my lesson by now."

"I'll take her upstairs and get her into bed," said Letty, taking charge, "I'll come and get you once she's settled." and she left the other two women in the drawing room.

Some time later, after a thorough examination by Letty and a treatment plan had been advised, Evangeline allowed Letty to bring her mother and grandmother up to see her.

When they entered the bedroom Evangeline was sitting up drinking some beef tea and Jessie was at her bedside where she had been throughout Letty's meticulous exami-nation. She smiled wanly at them and said, "Hello Mother, hello Grammie," in such a small voice that Louisa had wanted to cry. However, her mother-in-law threw her a warning look and she swallowed down her sobs and, pinning a smile to her face, she said, "Hello Evangeline, how are you feeling my dear?"

"I'm tired and very weak, but Aunt Letty is going to get me better." She turned to Letty with a grateful smile.

"Yes, a lot of rest and good food to build you up," said Letty, encouragingly.

Louisa leaned over her daughter and kissed her fore-head, "That's good to hear dear," she said, "we'll go now and let you rest and I'll drop in tomorrow and see how you're doing."

This was obviously the right thing to say as Evangeline rewarded her with a big smile.

Only when the three older women had gone did she allow herself to sink back on the pillows exhausted by the effort she had made for her mother and grandmother. Letty was allowed to know the depth that Evangeline had sunk to, physically and emotionally, but she promised not to divulge this to the others.

Over the next few weeks Evangeline improved due to the good care given her by Jessie and Letty. She had brief visits from Louisa who, she noticed, seemed to be having some difficulty walking, but Louisa had dismissed it as a combination of a damp spring and getting older.

Towards the end of her convalescence Jessie brought up the subject of her return to prison.

"Evie, Ah can feel it in ma bones that they'll be comin' for ye soon tae take ye back tae gaol. Would ye no' consider daein' a runner? Ah could try smugglin'ye oot disguised as Maggie," she said, "we baith ken lots of suffragettes had evaded goin' back tae prison by escaping through back doors disguised as domestic servants or hidden in laundry hampers."

"No Jess," Evangeline replied, with her old fervour, "I'll go back when they come for me and go on hunger strike immediately and I shall, in all probability, see you within a week or ten days. and we'll continue with this charade until I've served my remaining twenty-two days."

Jessie sighed and said, "A'right Evie, you ken best."

"I do Jess, you don't want them adding time to my sentence when they finally track me down after being on the run. That's what's happening, you know."

"That settles it then," replied Jessie, "let's go for a walk, it's a lovely day oot there."

It was just as they came through the gate of number 8 Lauder Road, almost a month after her release, that a plain-clothes detective approached them and issued the warrant for Evangeline's re-arrest and imprisonment.

She gave Jessie a quick hug and said, "Will you go back and let Grammie know I'm off again Jess, see you soon," and she went into the detective's waiting carriage in good spirits.

And so Evangeline went back to the Calton Gaol on the twentieth of May to serve as many days as she could before becoming so weak that she would be released again.

38

SUNDAY 25TH MAY 1913

E vangeline was released again on Sunday the twenty-fifth of May and this time she had a hacking cough which alarmed Jessie as they drove back to Lauder Road.

"In some ways ye're mair ill than the last time ye got released Evie, an' that wis wi' a' the force-feeding ye went through." Jessie said, looking very worried.

Between bouts of coughing Evangeline managed to say, "I think I might have a chest infection Jess, it's very damp in the gaol." She was shivering uncontrollably despite the warm May morning.

"They should've let ye oot sooner Evie," said Jessie angry at such neglect by the prison doctor, "ye've got a fever." She drew Evangeline to her to try to warm her chilled body.

"Telephone Aunt Letty when we get home Jess."

Just then, the cab came to a halt at number 8 and Jessie paid the driver and helped Evangeline out of the cab.

Her grandmother had been watching for their arrival and opened the door immediately. She was shocked by Evangeline's poor state of health. She said, "Her room is all ready for her Jessie, and there's a fire on and hot water bottles in her bed." Evangeline was coughing again and struggled to catch her breath. Eventually she managed to say, "Hello Grammie, would you telephone for Aunt Letty, I don't feel so well."

Charlotte and Jessie exchanged looks and Jessie nodded, as if agreeing that Evangeline must, indeed, be ill if she was asking for medical attention.

"You take Evangeline up and get her settled," said the old lady, "I'll telephone Letty."

As Jessie helped Evangeline upstairs she could hear Charlotte's hushed, but urgent, tone as she spoke to her daughter.

Letty arrived ten minutes later and Charlotte, who had been waiting near the door opened it and said, "Thank you for coming so quickly Letty dear, she's in a very bad way, worse than the last time and I'm worried she may even have to go to hospital."

Her mother's words alarmed Letty since she'd always known her to be calm in a crisis. "I'll go straight up Mother, don't worry, if it's possible, we'll care for her here," and she hurried upstairs carrying the Gladstone bag that her parents had given her as a graduation present over twenty years earlier.

Twenty minutes later Letty entered the drawing room where her mother was pacing up and down, a deep frown of worry creasing her forehead.

"Come and sit down Mother," Letty gently persuaded, "and I'll tell you about Evangeline and what I'm going to do."

Her mother sat on the sofa next to her and asked, "Is she going to be alright Letty? Does she need to go to hospital?"

and the question that she couldn't bring herself to ask was, "is she going to die?"

Calmly, Letty told Charlotte about how ill Evangeline was. "She has bronchitis Mother and, hopefully, they've released her in time before it has a chance to develop into pneumonia. This condition didn't develop overnight so the prison medical officer must not have been keeping a close eye on how the hunger strike was affecting her health." She paused, thinking that she would be writing a strongly-worded letter to the authorities.

"I'm going to get a specialist chest nurse in to look after Evangeline and I'll call in twice a day," she explained to her mother. "The main thing, at the moment, is to get her temperature down and I've prescribed ipecac and laudanum. The nurse will do some physical therapy to help clear her chest."

"So, she will recover then, won't she Letty?" her mother asked, still worried, despite Letty's words.

"I am confident that she will make a full recovery," she reassured her mother, "although the next twenty-four hours will be critical. I'll arrange for the nurse to come in this afternoon," she added.

"Thank you Letty dear," said her mother, finally feeling some relief, "I was so afraid we'd lose her. I don't know what I'd do without Evangeline, we've become very close in the time she's been staying here."

"I know Mother, but Evangeline, more so than some of my patients, has been well fed all of her life and her body is basically very strong," Letty said. "However, she has had a bit of a scare, so much so that she said it would be alright for Charles and Louisa to come and see her."

Charlotte smiled for the first time since Evangeline

entered the house and said, "She certainly has had a fright Letty, I'll go up and see her now."

"I'll telephone Wilf to get the details for the nurse and, after I've arranged that I'll call Charles and Louisa, although Charles may already have left for London."

Charles was, in fact, not leaving until later that afternoon and he and Louisa visited Evangeline who was being well cared for by a middle-aged, no nonsense-looking nurse.

All disapproval of their daughter's militant activities was set aside and the visit went well. Evangeline even asked her mother if she would come and see her the next day.

Jessie did not leave Evangeline's bedside for the first thirty-six hours and, only after the fever had finally broken, would she agree to rest in the guest room that Charlotte had made ready for her.

Letty was as good as her word and went in to see Evangeline in the mornings and evenings. On her visit the following Thursday she said, "Your lungs are healing well Evangeline and you are greatly improved over all."

Evangeline was sitting in an armchair and she had a healthy glow in her cheeks. "Thank you Aunt Letty, between you, Jessie and Nurse MacIntosh," she smiled at the nurse, "I have had the best care any patient could have asked for."

Letty sensed a change in Evangeline's personality, she was softer somehow, not the strident suffragette of before. Sometimes near-death experiences produced a profound change in people, she reflected.

She smiled and said, "You're very welcome Evangeline and I"m sure I speak for Nurse MacIntosh too. I don't think I need to see you again today, but I'll come by around noon tomorrow." She kissed her niece on the cheek, then she spoke to the nurse, "May I have a word with you please Nurse MacIntosh?"

The nurse followed Letty out onto the landing and, as she had expected, Letty said, "I want to thank you, you have done wonderful work with my niece but, as you can see, she no longer needs specialist care. If ever you need it, I'll be more than happy to write a testimonial for you."

After Letty and the nurse had gone Evangeline said to Jessie, "Jessie dear, I'm well and truly on the mend, although I'm by no means well enough to return to prison, so you don't have to be here all the time you know, and I was wondering what you think about an idea I have."

"What's that Evie?" Jessie asked, a bit disappointed that Evangeline didn't want her there all of the time.

"I need to keep on top of the escalation of our campaign of militancy," Evangeline explained, "and now that I'm feeling a bit better I thought it would be a good idea for you to be in the office in the mornings and then bring work here that we can both do in the afternoons. What do you think?"

Glad that she wasn't being banished and that Evangeline wasn't tiring of her company, she replied brightly, "That's an excellent plan Evie, Ah think ye're probably well enough tae dae two or three hours work in the afternoons. Besides, ye dinnae want tae step oot o' the front door since ye'll be arrested right away and ye're certainly no' well enough tae face the gaol, no for a wee while yet. Ah've noticed one o' thae sneaky detectives hingin' aboot, actin' as if he wis a normal person walkin' doon the road but spendin' a bit too long in passin' by number 8."

They both laughed, "They think they're clever, don't they Jess?"

"Aye Evie, but they'd have tae get up gey early tae keep up wi' suffragettes right enough," chuckled Jessie.

And so, this was the pattern of their days, Jessie would arrive with WSPU paperwork, carried in a large shopping bag so as not to alert the detectives that if Evangeline was fit enough to work, she must be fit enough to go back to prison, and the pair of them would work, happily, in Charlotte's study. Her grandmother had agreed to this arrangement on condition that Evangeline stayed in bed, resting in the mornings. The study window did not face the road so Evangeline would not be seen doing work and subsequently re-arrested.

Letty was coming in only twice a week now, but she wouldn't certify Evangeline was fit for work, or prison, until she was satisfied that her niece had recovered her former robust state of health.

By the end of May the escalation of suffragette attacks on property, letter bombs, arson and explosions had reached such a scale that some newspapers carried a 'weekly round-up' of the incidents perpetrated. These acts, the reports claimed, were driven by the leaders of the Women's Social and Political Union.

In 1913 Christabel Pankhurst wrote, "If men use explosives and bombs for their own purpose they call it war, and the throwing of a bomb that destroys other people is then described as a glorious and heroic deed. Why should a woman not make use of the same weapons as men. It is not only war we have declared. We are fighting for a revolution."

When the *Scotsman* published its weekly round-up of attacks, which had been very quickly dubbed *suffragette outrages*, Evangeline would read the reports to Jessie and sometimes, when innocent people got hurt, they would discuss, between themselves, the dubious wisdom of the WSPU 'generals'.

"Ah'm no' comfortable wi' people gettin' burnt wi' letter bombs or hurt in other ways Evie," said Jessie "an' Ah cannae help thinkin' aboot Mrs Pankhurst's words at the

Royal Albert Hall last October when, and I quote, "It has never been, nor will it ever be, the policy of the Women's Social and Political Union to endanger human life." Do you remember that Evie?"

"I do Jess, and the part where she said any recklessness was to our own lives and that was true, especially what we all went through with force-feeding," agreed Evangeline, "and I can't help wondering if they've somehow lost their way."

"Aye Evie, Ah ken what ye mean, things have changed drastically since then. Ah mean you only damaged a portrait, even if it wis a portrait o' the King, ye were never actually gonnae hurt another person wi' slashin a paintin', were ye?"

"No Jess, you're right. The Pankhursts are running the WSPU like an army with them as the generals and us as the soldiers who must obey orders and not take matters into our own hands."

"Aye, they wernae very happy wi' Emily Wilding Davison daein' things o' her ain accord, withoot askin' permission."

"That's why so many women left to join the Women's Freedom League and, in some ways, I can understand that they would want to be part of a democratically run organisation."

"Aye," agreed Jessie, "an' maybe that's what triggered this conversation we're havin' now. Ah'm jist no' happy that people are startin' tae get hurt, ye ken. Ah dinnae care aboot rich people's property, especially that belongin' tae the Liberal Government and MP's, yer ain family excepted of course, Evie."

"I suppose we need only take actions that we're comfortable with Jess," replied Evangeline, "after all, that's what Mrs

Pankhurst meant in her speech last year when she said
something like, "those of you who can express your militancy by breaking windows, do so", or words to that effect."

"Ah suppose so Evie, though now Ah'm seriously
wonderin' if, like the papers say, it'll turn people against us."

"It's certainly hard to know Jess. Now let's get on with
planning actions that we know won't result in people getting
hurt."

39

4TH JUNE 1913

T he following Wednesday afternoon, just as Jessie was packing up to go home Charlotte knocked and came into the study. Evangeline and Jessie looked up, surprised, since she never interrupted them while they were working.

On seeing her grim expression, Evangeline asked, "What is it Grammie? What's wrong?"

She handed the *Evening News* to Evangeline and said, "I thought you should see this."

then she walked out of the room without another word. Evangeline unfolded the newspaper and both she and Jessie were horrified as they read the headlines.

"SUFFRAGETTE SERIOUSLY INJURED AS SHE RUNS IN FRONT OF KING'S HORSE AT EPSOM DERBY

A WOMAN, carrying a flag with the suffragette colours of purple, white and green, ran out in front of the King's horse, Anmer, as it rounded the final bend of the Epsom Derby this afternoon. It is thought that she was trying to put the flag around the horse's neck. She was struck by the horse and knocked to the ground unconscious.

The horse fell, rolling over the jockey, also unconscious and who was taken to the race course's ambulance station where he later regained consciousness.

Spectators, including a doctor and a nurse ran onto the course to the aid of the seriously injured woman. The woman, who was later named as Emily Wilding Davison, was taken to the nearby Epsom Cottage Hospital where she is still unconscious.

The police believe Miss Davison was acting alone since there was no evidence of a wider suffragette presence at the race course.

We will bring our readers updated news bulletins on this incident as, and when, we have them."

"OH MY GOD EVANGELINE!" said a white-faced Jessie, "what an awfy thing tae dae!"

"It's terrible Jess, I just hope she recovers from her injuries," replied Evangeline, "but it sounds from what the newspaper says, that she's very seriously injured."

"She's a brave wummin," said Jessie, "always has been and so dedicated to the cause."

"We'll just have to hope and pray that she makes a full recovery," said Evangeline, sadly.

"The polis think she wis actin' alone, isn't that jist what we were talkin' aboot last week Evie?"

"It is," replied Evangeline, "and on that subject, I don't think even Mrs Pankhurst would have sanctioned such a dangerous act."

Emily Wilding Davison died four days later, on the 8th

of June, from a fracture at the base of her skull, despite having been operated on.

By the following week Evangeline was well, having fully recovered from the bronchitis, and she and Jessie had decided to make the trip to London to take part in the procession of mourners at Miss Davison's funeral.

The funeral was being held on Saturday the 14th of June and they had booked tickets on the 10am *Flying Scotsman,* on the Wednesday before, and had planned to stay with Amelia Wainwright again, as they had done on other occasions.

Evangeline was just finishing breakfast when her grandmother came into the dining room.

"Good morning Grammie," said Evangeline brightly, "it's a fine morning for travelling, although I wish the circumstances were not so tragic."

"I know dear and I'm glad that the inquest verdict was accidental death and not suicide as some people had been speculating."

"Of course it wasn't suicide Grammie," replied Evangeline quickly, "didn't she have a return ticket to London for later that afternoon, as well as a ticket for the WSPU dance that evening?"

"Yes Evangeline, those don't sound like the actions of a woman who intends to kill herself," Charlotte said. "What time is Jessie arriving with the cab?"

"She'll be here at nine-fifteen, that should give us sufficient time to get to the platform and find our carriage. We already have our tickets."

"Well just you take care dear, I don't want you getting arrested in London," the old lady cautioned.

"Don't worry Grammie, the London police won't recognise me, I'm just a small fish down there," she replied, smiling fondly at her grandmother.

Just then the doorbell rang and Evangeline got up saying, "That'll be Jessie now, I'll just fetch my coat and hat. My bag is already at the door." She kissed her grandmother and left the room.

Jessie was waiting on the doorstep and they hugged briefly. "Have you got everything Evie?" asked Jessie.

"I have, let's go." replied Evangeline.

Just as she was about to step into the cab, a man stepped between Evangeline and Jessie. It was a detective with a warrant for her re-arrest.

Jessie was shocked and disappointed, but it was a contingency she thought might materialise, with detectives spying on the house.

"Ah'll no' go withoot ye Evie, Ah'll jist go back tae the office," she said, putting a restraining hand on the detective's arm as he tried to hurry Evangeline away.

"One moment please," Evangeline said to the man, pulling her arm free, "I'm coming with you but we need a minute to talk."

Reluctantly he moved away a few paces, but kept his eyes fixed on the two women.

"I did think for a minute there that we could make a getaway, but they'd only intercept me at some point between here and London," Evangeline spoke quickly and quietly. "No Jess, you must keep to our arrangements and go to the funeral on behalf of the Edinburgh branch. You can tell me all about it when I come home again."

"A'right Evie," said Jessie, sadly, "Ah'll dae what ye say but it'll no' be the same on ma own."

"Chin up Jess," replied Evangeline, "now give me a kiss and get going, you don't want to miss the train. Tell Amelia why I'm not there."

Jessie kissed her and got into the cab. She waved to Evangeline as she wiped the tears from her eyes.

The detective approached her again just as her grandmother came up the path. Charlotte said, "I'll take your bag Evangeline, you won't need it where you're going," and she watched as her granddaughter was led to the waiting motor car.

JESSIE DID GO to the funeral procession and she felt the occasion was particularly sad, more so as she didn't have Evangeline by her side. She did, however, have Amelia Wainwright for company so she didn't feel totally out of place in such a big and crowded city.

Emily Davison's body was transported from Epsom to London and a small delegation met the coffin off the train at Victoria train station. They were joined by rank, upon rank, of five thousand women wearing the Women's Social and Political Union colours of purple, white and green. The principle mourners from the organisation, who led the procession, were dressed in white.

Jessie and Amelia walked arm in arm, behind the horse-drawn hearse as it made its slow, two hour journey through the streets of London. Fifty thousand people lined the streets to watch it pass by. There was a short service at St George's Church in Bloomsbury, then the coffin was transported to King's Cross station, where it would be taken by train to the Northumberland town of Morpeth, which was Emily's home town. A guard of honour from the Women's Social and Political Union accompanied her on her final journey home.

In Morpeth, around a hundred suffragettes followed the

coffin from Morpeth station to the church and thousands lined the streets there. Only a few suffragettes were allowed in the churchyard as the funeral and burial were private.

Like Evangeline, Mrs Pankhurst was meant to be in the funeral procession but she was arrested that morning under the Cat and Mouse Act, to continue serving her sentence.

40

WEDNESDAY 18TH JUNE 1913

L ouisa and Charles were seated in Professor Duncan's consulting room, waiting to hear about the results of X-rays which Louisa had recently undergone. She had been suffering from pain in her legs which had been getting progressively worse over the past few months.

After consulting Wilf Cunningham at the Salisbury Medical Practice, she had been referred to the Edinburgh Royal Infirmary for preliminary tests and X-rays. Both she and Charles were lost in their own thoughts when Professor Duncan entered the room carrying the X-ray plates which he laid on his desk.

Before sitting down, he said, "Good morning Lady Frobisher, Sir Charles," shaking their hands, "I have asked you to come and see me today so that I can explain the results of your recent X-ray investigation."

Taking Louisa's hand in his, Charles said, not so much puzzled but deeply worried, "Yes, Professor Duncan, but I had expected the results to be sent to Dr Cunningham who referred my wife for the X-rays."

Charles had been worried since the hospital appointment letter, asking Louisa to attend a consultation with Professor Duncan, had arrived although he had kept his concerns to himself.

"Quite, Sir Charles," replied the consultant kindly, "and he will receive that information after our meeting today."

For the first time Louisa grew uneasy. Up until now she had believed, as Wilf had thought, that she probably had some form of arthritis and that the X-rays had been carried out to confirm this.

"Do I have arthritis Professor Duncan?" she asked.

Professor Duncan looked at husband and wife and got up from behind his desk and placed the X-ray plates on the the X-ray reader on the wall and he switched on the light behind them.

Charles gave an involuntary gasp when the professor switched on the light since he knew, without a shadow of a doubt, what he was looking at. He squeezed Louisa's hand and she looked at him in alarm, then she looked at the unsmiling face of the consultant.

"What?" she asked, looking from one to the other, "what is it? What is wrong with my legs?"

Professor Duncan sat down and clasped his hands lightly on the desk. He cleared his throat and said, "Lady Frobisher, I'm sorry to have to tell you that you have osteosarcoma." On seeing her uncomprehending expression, he added, "you have bone cancer."

She turned slowly and looked at Charles. "Cancer?" she whispered the question, "Am I going to die Charles?" she asked more firmly.

"I cannot answer that question with precision at this time, my dear," the professor said gently, "but there is a treatment which might shrink the cancer, or at least slow its spread to other parts of your body. It is called radiation therapy and it has been shown to slow the growth of cancerous cells."

Louisa sat clutching Charles's hand, silent tears streaming down her face.

"Do you have a clear treatment plan for my wife, Professor?" Charles asked.

"Yes Sir Charles," he replied, then addressing Louisa, he said, "Lady Frobisher, I would advocate three treatments a week for four weeks, after which time we will X-ray you again and see what progress has been made."

"Will the radiation be painful?" she asked, taking a deep breath and straightening her shoulders, at which a great sense of relief surged through Charles. He recognised this determined mannerism of hers and he was relieved that she was going to work with the treatment and not against it.

"No, it won't be painful my dear," replied the professor kindly, "you will only be exposed to the radiation for a few minutes per treatment. However, it may produce some unpleasant side effects."

Charles, who had not practised medicine for some years and who was not up to date with the latest practices in cancer treatment, asked, "Such as?"

"The treatment may cause vomiting and diarrhoea Lady Frobisher. There is also a possibility of your hair thinning, or even some hair loss," he said, looking into Louisa's wide eyes.

When he said this, her hand went involuntarily and unconsciously to her head. Louisa's hair was her crowning glory and always had been. Then she asked, "And what if I don't have the radiation treatment, what will happen then?" Charles looked at her, shocked at the idea that she might refuse the treatment.

The professor was silent for a few moments, weighing up his words carefully, then with great solemnity, he said, "Without treatment my dear, I don't believe you would survive to see Christmas."

"I see," said Louisa, shocked to the core to think that she might have so little time left.

"Despite the unpleasant side effects, the radiation will also help to reduce the pain you have been experiencing, which would only become more severe in the absence of any treatment."

Louisa nodded her understanding and said, "Then I shall undergo the radiation treatment. When do I begin Professor?"

"I will get the process under way today and you will receive word by last post on Friday, at the latest. I should think everything should be in place for your treatment to commence on Monday next. Does that give you sufficient time to make arrangements for your stay in hospital?"

Both Charles and Louisa were dismayed, as neither had thought it would involve a hospital admission. Louisa said, "Oh, I hadn't realised I would have to stay in hospital. I rather thought that since the duration of the treatment is only a few minutes, that it would be on an outpatient basis." She sounded disappointed and felt overwhelmed by everything she had heard since entering the professor's consulting room. "I thought I would be able to continue working," she added lamely.

"It's best you stay in hospital so we can monitor you and treat any side-effects, at least for the first few treatments," he said with empathy, "It will all feel very alien to you at first."

"Very well Professor," Louisa replied, "I will make the necessary arrangements and await your letter confirming everything."

"Do either of you have any further questions?" the consultant asked.

"No, thank you," Louisa replied.

"Not at the moment Professor Duncan," said a subdued Charles.

The professor stood up and shook hands with them both, signalling that the consultation was over. "Thank you for coming in, I will see you again in due course. Goodbye Lady Frobisher, Sir Charles."

"Goodbye Professor Duncan," they both replied as they left the room.

THEY GOT into Charles's black Daimler, a recent purchase, and both of them sat in stunned silence for several minutes, then Charles spoke. "Louisa my darling, I am so very sorry that this is happening to you," then he banged his fist on the steering wheel and said angrily, "It's so unfair! You're a good, kind and generous woman, this shouldn't be happening to you."

She looked at him and saw tears running down his cheeks. She gently brushed them away and said, "I'm sorry too, Charles, but it has happened and we will just have to get through this together, like we have with everything else."

He looked at her in wonder and stroked her soft cheek. "Louisa you are the most amazing and strong woman I have ever met. I do admire your courage my dear."

"Take me home please Charles. I have much to see to, for our dinner party this evening."

Charles's jaw dropped when he realised he had totally forgotten, with all that had just happened, that this was

Louisa's fifty-fifth birthday and their twenty-seventh wedding anniversary.

"Oh my dear Louisa!" he exclaimed, "it had totally gone from my mind with the news we have just received. Don't you think we should cancel it, under the circumstances?"

"No Charles, I think we should go ahead with it and we won't tell anyone our news, not today anyway," she said, firmly, "There will be time enough at the weekend when we will visit both sets of parents and tell them then."

"If you're sure Louisa?"

"I'm sure Charles, I want to make the most of our time as normally as possible, before the radiation affects my life for the next month or so."

"Then let's go home my dear," replied Charles, patting her on the knee.

41

THAT EVENING

C harles marvelled at the way Louisa was able to act as if she had never received any life-changing news that morning and was her usual sociable, happy self.

He wasn't finding it quite so easy and was often distracted and had to be repeatedly called back from his preoccupation with Louisa's diagnosis, failing to answer when being asked a question.

"What's wrong with you this evening Charles?" his mother asked, after it had happened a couple of times.

Louisa looked at him warningly, she didn't want him to disclose their news this evening, not when everything was going so well. Even Evangeline was on her best behaviour for her mother's birthday and her parents' anniversary. She had been released once more under the Cat and Mouse Act and was beginning to recover well from her hunger strike and she would likely be re-arrested at any time over the coming days or weeks to complete the remaining period of her three month sentence.

"Sorry Mother," he said, looking apologetic, "just politics, I've got a few things on my mind, but I'll put them to one side now." He beamed a huge smile at her, which didn't for one second convince Louisa.

There were six guests altogether; Louisa's parents, Lord and Lady Moncrieff, Charles's mother, Charlotte Frobisher, Evangeline, and Letty and Wilf Cunningham. They had all brought little gifts for Louisa and, after his mother's admonition, Charles managed to get into the celebration, even taking part in a hilarious game of charades.

Later on, in bed, Charles held Louisa close, not wanting to let go of his precious wife. During the afternoon, while Louisa was busy with the flower arranging for the dining table, Charles had taken himself off to the Medical School library to do some research on bone cancer. His reading had not been reassuring, hence his distraction during the celebratory meal.

Louisa's prognosis did not look good. Even if the radiation slowed down the growth of the cancer, it was possible that it had already spread to one or more organs. The best outcome, as far as he could determine, was a one to two years survival period.

He had thought of little else for the rest of the day and, in fact, he had not been lying to his mother earlier, since he had made the decision to step down as Member of Parliament for Edinburgh South and use the time to be with Louisa for however long she had left.

As she lay in his arms, he stroked her lovely hair and said, "I've made a decision Louisa dear."

"Yes Charles," she said sleepily, "what's that?"

"I'm standing down as MP so I can look after you. I'll telephone Asquith in the morning and he can start the proceedings for a by-election. I'll leave at the end of the month."

All sleepiness vanished and Louisa sat up. "But you can't Charles, it's your job, your career." she said.

"And you're my wife Louisa, you are more important than any career. You may need the services of a physician over the coming months and I wouldn't trust anyone else to look after you, my precious girl." He drew her to him and kissed her fondly on the lips.

Louisa replied, "Alright Charles, it will be good to have you at home all the time and we can go for drives if my legs won't let me walk or cycle."

"Good, that's settled then. Try to get some sleep my darling."

"I think I'll tell Letty tomorrow Charles. I think I shall need her support in the days and weeks to come. Good-night, sleep well," she said, settling down again.

"You too, Louisa, goodnight." But it was a long time before he fell into a troubled sleep.

42

THE FOLLOWING DAY
THURSDAY 19TH JUNE

W hen Letty heard Louisa's serious request, on the telephone that morning, to meet her, she knew it must be something important since Louisa never disturbed her during working hours.

"Are you alright Louisa?" asked Letty, "you don't sound very well. Are your legs still giving you pain?"

"It's my legs I want to talk to you about Letty, are you able to come here at eleven o'clock?"

"Yes, of course dear girl," Letty replied immediately, I can come now if you prefer," she offered.

"No, no eleven will be fine. I'll have a pot of tea ready, see you soon," and she put the receiver gently back into its cradle.

She hadn't slept well and she couldn't help thinking that she might be more seriously ill, than she first thought, if Charles had made the decision to step down as MP since he really enjoyed his work and he was very good at it, she thought worriedly.

She was in the drawing room when Maggie announced Letty's arrival. It was a beautiful day and a fragrant summer breeze was coming in through the open window. Louisa pinned a smile to her face and stood up to embrace her best friend. "It's too lovely a day to be be sharing bad news," she thought to herself and wondered, for the tenth time that morning, if she was doing the right thing.

"Would you bring the tea in now please Maggie?" she said before Maggie had closed the door.

"Certainly Lady Frobisher," she said chattily, "Ah've got yer favrite shortbread tae, jist oot o' the oven," and then she was gone.

"Bless her," Louisa thought to herself, smiling, "a touch of normality in my upside-down world today." Out loud, she said, "Sit down Letty, I hope I haven't taken you away from too many patients."

"Not at all, it's a quiet day and Wilf will manage admirably," she replied, then looking at Louisa's legs she added, "How are the legs Louisa? I thought you were walking a little stiffly last night"

Just then, Maggie came in with a tray laden with china teapot, cups and plates and a plate of delicious-smelling warm shortbread. She put it on the low table in front of the sofa where Louisa and Letty were seated and asked, "Shall I pour Lady Frobisher?" Maggie always asked this question, ever-hopeful of hearing snippets of her employer's conversation.

"Not today Maggie, I'll do it myself, but thank you for offering though."

"Ye're welcome," said Maggie cheerfully, she was never offended if Louisa wanted to pour the tea herself.

Letty regarded her friend as she poured the tea and noticed the dark circles under her eyes. When Louisa handed her the cup and saucer she said, "You look pale and tired this morning Louisa, are you sure you are alright?"

Louisa left her tea untouched and turned to Letty, hands clasped in her lap. "Actually, I'm not alright Letty, I have bone cancer."

Letty's cup, which was half way to her lips, clattered back onto the saucer and she put it down on the table so quickly that some of it spilled into the saucer. Her blue eyes were wide as she took Louisa's hands in hers. She was aware of how cold they were, despite the warmth of the June morning. "Your legs?" was all she could utter. "But when ... how long ... you didn't say anything last night," she stumbled over her words.

Louisa told her about the appointment with Professor Duncan at the Royal Infirmary the previous day and that she and Charles had decided not to tell anyone until they had got used to the idea themselves.

"We'll tell both sets of parents this weekend, but I don't want Evangeline knowing just yet," Louisa explained.

Letty, still reeling from the shock, merely nodded.

"I wanted you to know as soon as possible Letty as I am in need of your support. I didn't sleep well last night, as you would imagine, and I'm having difficulty assimilating the information, to be perfectly honest with you."

"But, last night Louisa?' Letty shook her head in disbelief, "You seemed so normal, so happy ..." her voice trailed off.

"I know, I just wanted to have a normal dinner since I don't know how long it will be before I feel normal or well again."

Letty hugged Louisa and said, "Dear Louisa, I am so very sorry to hear this news, but you know, they're getting some very good results with radiation therapy and I've heard that Professor Duncan is the best. Did he give you a prognosis?"

"No, he couldn't tell at this point in time," she replied,

beginning to feel a little better after what Letty said about the treatment and her consultant. "They will take more X-rays after the twelve treatment sessions to see if it has shrunk the cancer. I'm not looking forward to the side effects though, they sound awful." She pulled a face.

"I'll make you some ginger tea and bring it to you in hospital and when you get home again. It works wonders for nausea, you know," Letty promised her.

"Thank you Letty, you are so kind. Professor Duncan said that Wilf will receive a letter with the X-rays results and diagnosis, but you can tell him now, if you like." She sat back and drank her, now almost cold tea, then she picked up a bit of shortbread, saying, "I actually feel like this now. Drink up your tea Letty and I'll pour you a fresh cup, the teapot is still warm."

"I did think you were getting thinner Louisa, but I didn't connect that with the pain in your legs, some doctor I am," she said with a self-deprecating smile.

"Nonsense Letty! Neither did Charles. I suppose it's not the first thing you think about when it's a spouse or a friend. It's different with your patients in your consulting room, you're a step removed, so to speak."

"How do you feel about the possibility of your hair getting thin or even falling out?" asked Letty. "I know how you feel about your beautiful hair Louisa and with good reason."

She patted her hair and said, "I know it's just vanity, but I think that's what I'm dreading most. I have only just come to terms with going grey at the temples," she laughed and said, "Vanity thy name is woman!" as was said of Lady Lilith in Rossetti's painting.

"As if you don't get vain men!" exclaimed Letty, "I've seen some real peacocks over the years, I assure you." They both laughed and, suddenly, the atmosphere was lighter and Louisa felt almost like her old self again.

"Thank you so much for coming to see me Letty," she said, "I feel much better about it all and I know I can tell you anything - even my deepest fears that I wouldn't tell Charles about."

"I'll do everything I can to help you Louisa, just let me know how I can help, anytime."

"I will Letty dear, now I must let you get back to work, it's almost noon and I'm sure Wilf could do with your help."

Both women stood up and embraced. "I'll see you to the door," said Louisa, "and thank you again."

She stood in the doorway and waved, as her friend walked up the road, back to the Salisbury Medical Practice.

43

EDINBURGH ROYAL INFIRMARY

JULY 1913

Louisa's last radiation treatment was on Friday the eighteenth of July, exactly one month after the shock diagnosis and, to her relief, she only had to stay in hospital for the first week's treatment.

Letty, true to her word, brought Louisa the ginger tea but she was fortunate in that the worst of that side effect only lasted whilst she was an inpatient, where they treated the unpleasant bouts of nausea.

As she waited for Charles to collect her, she thought back to the weekend following her diagnosis, when she and Charles went to tell her parents and Charles's mother.

Charles had offered to speak to them for her but she insisted that she would do that herself, with him by her side.

Evangeline had been re-arrested two days after the celebratory dinner party and had been released and re-arrested again since then.

She and Charles had gone, firstly, to her parents house in Heriot Row and, as they sat having tea in the drawing room, Louisa mentally prepared herself for the talk ahead. She had asked her mother to make sure her father would be at home and, although Emily Moncrieff hadn't voiced it, she had felt a pang of concern. She knew about Louisa's legs giving her pain and that had been making walking difficult for her daughter, but she was totally unprepared for her daughter's news.

Lady Moncrieff had poured the tea and there had been some smalltalk about the weather etcetera. Louisa took Charles's hand in hers and took a deep breath.

"Mother, Father," she said, "I'm afraid I have some worrying news."

Both her parents put their cups and saucers down on the low table between the two sofas where Charles and Louisa sat opposite .

"I have bone cancer and I am about to undergo a course of radiation therapy which will commence on Monday. It has been shown to shrink cancerous tumours, so we are hoping for the best outcome." Her prepared little speech over with, she looked at Charles who nodded agreement.

Her parents sat in stunned silence. They had almost lost Louisa to complications after giving birth to Evangeline more than twenty years ago and they were afraid that she might now be taken from them by this terrible disease.

Eventually, her mother found her voice and she asked, "When, or how, will they know if the treatment is successful?" She looked from Louisa to Charles.

"I will have more X-rays taken after the course is finished and Professor Duncan, he's my consultant," she explained, "will have a better idea of the prognosis then."

Her parents noticed that Charles wasn't saying much and that he didn't seem as hopeful as their daughter.

"What's your opinion on the matter Charles?" asked her father, "after all, you're still a doctor."

Charles chose his words carefully, not wanting to give

away anything that he had learned a few days before. "Well Henry, as you know, it's a long time since I practiced medicine and oncology was not my field. However, I can tell you that I am stepping down as Member of Parliament for Edinburgh South, at the end of the month, so I can be on hand to help Louisa and to be with her throughout this and any future treatment she might need."

"So you see, Mother and Father," Louisa broke in, "it's not as bad as you might think and Letty will be on hand too, so we're well organised." Her brightness didn't fool her mother, but she held her tongue, being accustomed to her daughter's method of coping.

"How long will this course of treatment last? And will you have to stay in hospital?" asked her mother.

"I'm to have three treatments a week for four weeks and I only have to stay in hospital for the first week or so, so they can monitor any side effects." Louisa replied.

Henry and Emily knew their daughter well and that she wouldn't want them to worry about her, so they tacitly agreed to go along with Louisa's hopeful and positive approach to it."

"Well, one week isn't so bad, is it?" said her mother, "and we can come and visit you, as will Charlotte and Letty, I'm sure."

"There is one thing Charles and I must ask of you both," Louisa said, hesitantly.

"Yes dear, what's that?" asked her mother.

"We don't want Evangeline to know about any of this, not yet anyway, not until after the treatment when we have a better idea about a prognosis," said Louisa.

"She's in and out of prison under this Cat and Mouse Act," Charles added, "and we don't want her to have to deal with Louisa's health as well."

"But won't she know?" asked Louisa's father, "I mean during the periods of release from prison?"

"No Henry," said Charles, "she lives with my mother, as you know, and is busy with campaign business when she's well enough."

"Very well Charles," Emily spoke for both of them, "You have our word, she won't hear about it from us."

They left shortly after and drove to Lauder Road to tell Charles's mother the news. By pre-arrangement, Letty agreed to be present in case his mother needed support.

They went through a similar conversation with Charlotte, although she took more convincing of the need to keep the news from Evangeline.

"She's not a child, Charles," she remonstrated with her son, "and perhaps it will give her a better perspective on what's important in life."

"Please, Mother-in-law," Louisa had begged, "let's just keep it between ourselves for now," and she looked at Charles and Letty. "That would be the most helpful thing you could do for me just now, until we have a better idea of the progress of the disease or, more hopefully, the success of the treatment."

"Very well Louisa," the older woman agreed, "I'll keep quiet about it, for now."

44

8 LAUDER ROAD

SUNDAY 3RD AUGUST 1913

I n the end it was Charlotte who told Evangeline about her mother's illness. She had finally completed her prison sentence, although it had taken her four stretches to do so. Charlotte didn't think that the treatment Louisa had undergone had done much to reduce the cancer, or the pain since her daughter-in-law seemed to be having even more difficulty walking and, although Louisa was trying hard to hide it, she knew that she was in considerable pain.

It was a quiet Sunday afternoon and, for once, Evangeline was home for Sunday lunch as she wasn't due to go out until the early evening.

They were having coffee in the drawing room when Evangeline said, "Oh Grammie, it is so good to know that I have finished that dreadful prison sentence which seems to have dragged on for ever, with all this Cat and Mouse business, and I can leave the house without worrying that I might be arrested at any moment."

"Yes dear, I would think you wouldn't want to get

arrested again for your militant activity any time soon," replied her grandmother, trying to sound nonchalant.

"But we must fight on Grammie," said Evangeline, "In fact we're having a special meeting tonight in Drummond Street, now that I am a free woman again. But I have no intention of being arrested since, although it does publicise the cause, it puts me out of action for too long." She stroked Rosie's velvety ears. Rosie, as usual, was lying on the sofa snuggling into Evangeline.

Charlotte said, "Evangeline dear, there is something I need to talk to you about."

"Yes Grammie?" she said absently, as she was thinking about the Edinburgh branch's next plan of action.

"Your mother is very ill dear, she has cancer," her grandmother told her gently, but bluntly, all the same.

She stopped stroking the hound's ears and sat up straight, giving her grandmother her full attention now. "What?" she asked, not comprehending, "Mother has cancer? But I thought her legs were sore due to arthritis." She shook her head, wondering if she was hearing things, "When was she diagnosed with this awful disease?"

"Actually, it was on her birthday in June that she and your father were told about it," said Charlotte, "Wilf had referred Louisa for X-rays to confirm what he thought was arthritis."

"June?" replied Evangeline hotly, "Why am I only being told about it now Grammie? Why didn't anyone tell me before? I suppose Grandmama and Grandpapa Moncrieff know too?" she asked indignantly.

"Of course they do and so do Letty and Wilf," replied Charlotte.

"So," said Evangeline, getting up and pacing the room, much to Rosie's dismay, "I am the only one not to know that my own mother has had a life-threatening disease for the past ..." she paused to do a quick calculation, "... six weeks."

"Evangeline my dear," said her grandmother, with a heavy sigh, "I was never in favour of keeping it from you, but your mother pleaded with me not to say anything. At the time it was thought that the treatment would kill the cancer cells, but I don't think it has. We'll know for certain when your mother sees the consultant again tomorrow, when she goes for the results of her most recent X-rays."

Evangeline was stunned into silence for a few moments, trying to take in this devastating news, then she said, "And that's another thing, how am I unaware of her going for treatment? How did I not notice?"

"Well dear," replied Charlotte, with a short mirthless laugh, "you have been in and out of prison and when you were out of that awful place, you were trying to recover your health."

A thought struck Evangeline, "I was aware of Mother looking older and pale when she visited me here," said Evangeline thoughtfully, "but I put that down to the stress and strain of me being ill and all the time it was my poor mother who has been ill." She stopped pacing and sat down heavily on the sofa and finally she started to cry, deep, gulping sobs that wracked her, still too thin, body.

Charlotte went over and sat on the arm of the sofa. She put her arm around Evangeline's shoulders and pulled her granddaughter to her, letting her cry while she uttered soothing words and stroked her hair.

Eventually the sobs subsided and she stopped crying. Her grandmother said, "I thought you should know Evangeline in case that, in the weeks or months to come, your mother's condition gets worse and you might be stuck in prison and unable to see her."

Another realisation hit her and she said, "So that's why Father stopped being an MP, and all this time I thought it was because of me," she said, shaking her head, incredulous. "I thought I had embarrassed him one time too many with my slashing of the King's portrait," she gave a self-deprecating laugh, "how egotistical and self-centred of me!"

"Charles wanted to be on hand and to spend as much time with your mother as possible," replied Charlotte, "I know my son Evangeline dear, and, although he hasn't actually said anything to me - or Louisa for that matter, I think he suspects the cancer is more advanced than the doctors first thought."

"Oh Grammie, what a mess I've made of things and I've been horrid to Mother and Father and acted like a spoiled brat." She shot up from the sofa and said, "I must go and see them immediately."

Charlotte caught her by the hand and said, "Don't go in all angry and accusing Evangeline, I beg of you, and before you do go I would advise you to go upstairs and bathe your red, swollen eyes dear," and she gave her granddaughter a weak smile. Evangeline nodded and left the room.

LATER THAT AFTERNOON Evangeline sat on her parents' sofa in the drawing room, holding Louisa's hand. A tearful reconciliation had taken place and Evangeline had apologised to both her parents for being the cause of so much worry. Even her father had relented, to a degree.

At first Charles and Louisa had been dismayed and annoyed that his mother had broken the news to Evangeline.

"Your grandmother promised me that she would not say

anything to you," Louisa had said, crossly, but Charles had intervened.

"Don't be cross with Mother, Louisa dear, Mother was right to tell Evangeline and perhaps we should have done so sooner," he said, then added, "It was just that there never seemed to be a good time Evangeline, with you in and out of prison under that damned Cat and Mouse Act."

Evangeline nodded, guilt flooding through her, and for the first time since joining the Women's Social and Political Union, a seed of doubt was sown.

"Please believe me when I say that I will not do anything to upset, worry or embarrass you from now on," she said solemnly.

Louisa looked at her, surprised, but it was Charles who asked directly, "Does that mean you intend to leave the Pankhurst's organisation?"

"No, I don't think so Father," she said, unsure, "but I won't be part of any direct militancy. I really have to consider matters carefully before I can say any more." Louisa and Charles looked at each other, a mix of relief and shock on their faces.

Evangeline stood up and said, "You're looking very tired Mother, I'll go and let you rest." She bent down and kissed Louisa's forehead.

"Before you go Evangeline," Charles said, a little embarrassed, "you're welcome to come back home, you know."

"Thank you Father," Evangeline replied, "that's kind of you, but I think I shall remain at Grammie's, it would be a wrench if I left now, she's got so used to having me there. Goodbye Mother, Father, I'll come and see you tomorrow evening and you can tell me about your appointment with Professor Duncan."

They both looked at her in surprise and she said, "Grammie told me about it." Then she was gone.

After a few moments silence Louisa said, "Charles, I think our daughter has finally grown up."

Postscript

OVER THE COMING days Evangeline gave a lot of thought to her position in the Women's Social and Political Union, especially with the, then, current escalation in arson and bombing attacks. She weighed this up carefully. Her abhorrence of people getting hurt and her promise to her parents that she would take no further part in the militant destruction of property led her to finally decide that her position, as a paid organiser of the Women's Social and Political Union, had become untenable.

She also wanted to be able to help people in her mother's situation and she decided to apply to the Medical School at Edinburgh University to continue studying for her medical degree. She was aware that this would do nothing to help her mother, or help to ease her pain now, but she hoped to help people in the future. Every member of her family was delighted with these decisions and the change in Evangeline herself.

45

EDINBURGH ROYAL INFIRMARY

FRIDAY, 24TH OCTOBER 1913

Miss Anderson, Professor Duncan's secretary, showed Louisa and Charles into his consulting room. "The Professor has asked me to pass on his apologies as he will be a few minutes late, having been called down to one of the wards. Please make yourself comfortable."

"Thank you," said Charles.

"Can I get you something to drink? Tea? Water?" she asked kindly.

"Water please," said Louisa, a bit breathlessly, after her slow and painful walk from the lift, even though that had been just a matter of ten yards or so.

By now, Louisa was using two walking sticks to get around, her legs had lost a lot of strength and the muscles were wasting away. Charles had tried, unsuccessfully, to persuade her to use a wheelchair, but she had determinedly refused.

The results of the X-rays she'd had taken after her first round of radiation treatment had not been encouraging since there was little difference in the tumour mass and she had been given the option of a further round which she had declined.

She had said to the consultant, "What would be the point Professor Duncan? If the first lot of treatment hasn't worked, I doubt if it would work the next time."

He had replied, "I'm afraid I have to agree with you Lady Frobisher, but some people find it psychologically beneficial, if not medically helpful." So the radiation therapy was discontinued and replaced by a monthly consultation to monitor the progress of the disease.

She was deep in thought when Professor Duncan entered the room and greeted them, "Good morning Lady Frobisher, Sir Charles," he said, shaking hands with Louisa first, and then Charles.

He sat down behind his desk and asked Louisa, "How are you feeling Lady Frobisher? How have you been since our last meeting?"

Louisa looked at Charles before replying and he simply nodded his encouragement for her to tell the doctor about the new symptoms.

"I'm afraid I'm getting very breathless Professor Duncan. I find that I can now hardly walk across the room without stopping to catch my breath."

"I see, anything else?" he asked, scrutinising her and seeing she had lost even more weight. Her face had hollows under the sharply defined cheek bones and his heart filled with sympathy for this dignified and courageous woman.

She went on, "Well, I'm having to use these all the time now," she said, holding up her walking sticks, "and my clothes are all too large for me but I'm reluctant to buy new ones in case ... in case," she faltered and looked down at her hands, trying hard not to cry. Charles took her hands in his and squeezed them affectionately. The gold wrist watch, which had fitted perfectly well when he had given it to her last Christmas, was hanging loose and in danger of falling off. She had recently stopped wearing her wedding and engagement rings lest they fell off and got lost. They had been stored safely in her jewellery box to be given to Evangeline in due course.

"Let's have a look at your latest X-rays now, Lady Frobisher," said the professor, getting up and attaching several X-ray plates along the wall. He switched on the light and Charles forced himself to look, dreading that they would confirm his fears. He had been watching Louisa become more and more ill as the weeks progressed and his heart was heavy. He did look up when he heard the professor speaking.

"As you can see," he said, pointing to various parts of the X-ray plates for Louisa's benefit, since he knew that Charles could read them plainly enough, "the disease has become rather aggressive since your last X-rays and has spread to your lungs - which accounts for your breathlessness - and to your liver I'm afraid."

Charles squeezed Louisa's hand again and asked the question he knew she wanted to ask, "In your opinion, how long has my wife got to live Professor Duncan?"

The professor sat down again and clasped his hands on the desk in front of him, in what they now realised, was a familiar gesture. His kind face was sad as he replied, "Well, it's hard to be precise, but I would say that you're looking at two to three months, perhaps less."

Louisa and Charles sat, stunned into silence. It was worse than Charles had thought. He was still holding Louisa's hands and he suddenly felt hot tears splashing onto his hands. He put his arm around her shoulders and drew her to him. She lay her head against his chest and wept bitterly.

"I'm so sorry Lady Frobisher, I wish, from the bottom of my heart, that I had better news than this for you both." Louisa stopped crying, sat up and straightened her shoulders, then she said, "Thank you Professor Duncan. I know that you have done everything in your power to help me and I appreciate your kindness and honesty." She was feeling exhausted now from the bad news and weeping, "And thank you for not giving me false hope. I just need to get used to the idea now." Then she turned to Charles and said, "Please take me home now Charles."

The professor got up and walked around his desk. He shook both their hands and said, "You are a very brave woman Lady Frobisher, goodbye. Goodbye Sir Charles."

Louisa didn't speak on the journey home, now that her tears had dried up she just felt numb. Once they were back in the house, Charles said, "Louisa, my darling girl, I am so dreadfully sorry and I don't know how I am going to live without you." Suddenly Charles was weeping, the tears that he'd been keeping back for so long, falling like torrents.

It was Louisa's turn to comfort him. She sat holding him in her arms, uttering soothing words in a low voice. When he finally stopped crying, she said, "Charles, I was thinking on the way home. I was thinking that deep down I knew this was always a possibility, I'd hoped not, but now it is more than just a possibility, it is happening. In the car I thought there is no point in railing against God; that won't give me the life I'm about to lose in the near future, ..."

"Oh Louisa my dear," Charles interrupted, but Louisa cut him off.

"No Charles, let me finish," she said, "I could spend whatever time I have left being angry and bitter, but that won't give me the life I am going to lose either. So I made a decision Charles, I am going to live each day I have left to the fullest of my ability and then, when I am no longer able to do that, I shall cherish each day as it comes. Now this is important, Charles, I want you to do the same. I want you to share each day with me, make the most of our time together. Then when I am no longer able to go outdoors, I would like you to read to me as the days grow shorter." This last request was so poignant, with its twin meaning, that Charles began to cry again.

"Come Charles," she chided, mildly, "there will be ample time for crying after."

Charles made a big effort and dried his tears, and, giving a soulful sigh, he replied, "Very well my dear Louisa, you are right, as always. Do you want me to tell the family soon?"

She thought about that for a few moments then said, "No Charles, I should prefer not. I should like to spend as much time, as possible, free from the sadness and pity of others. I'll know when the time is right and when it is, we shall tell them together."

"As you wish my darling," Charles replied.

"There is one good thing that has come out of all this," she said, brightening.

"What is that Louisa?" asked Charles, puzzled.

"That Evangeline has given up the Women's Social and Political Union and has returned to complete her medical degree."

"Yes, indeed," he agreed and kissed her gently on the lips.

46

ARTHUR'S SEAT

FRIDAY, 21ST NOVEMBER 1913

I t was one of those beautiful crisp, sunny mornings in November, the kind where the sky is a brilliant blue and the air is fresh with the scents of late autumn.

Louisa and Charles were sitting in their Daimler enjoying a picnic lunch. Charles had parked at a high vantage point by a flank of Arthur's Seat and they took in the panoramic view to the north, across the sparkling Firth of Forth, with the Kingdom of Fife beyond.

In her heart, Louisa knew this would be her last outing with Charles, since her health was failing and her energy was waning.

Over the four weeks, following her devastating prognosis, she and Charles had lived every day to the full. On one occasion Charles had driven them down the coast of East Lothian and they had stopped at the top of the Gullane sand dunes and they'd had their picnic lunch in the car as they looked out over the Forth estuary towards the North Sea,

Sometimes they ate in hotel restaurants but they mainly preferred to share an intimate picnic lunch parked in a picturesque spot. Maggie always provided a picnic basket full of tasty and nutritious food. She had a feeling that there was something going on with her employers but she couldn't put her finger on it.

Louisa had been eating less and less over the previous week or so, and almost nothing on the picnic today. As they drank coffee from a thermos flask Charles took surreptitious looks at Louisa. He too, was aware of her energy ebbing away and today there was an ethereal quality to her beautiful face. She looked so at peace with the world.

Aware that he was looking at her, she turned to him and smiled her radiant smile that had captivated his heart all those years ago.

She took his hand in hers and sighed. "Isn't it so beautiful up here Charles? I feel very close to heaven in these peaceful surroundings, serene almost."

"You look like serenity itself today, Louisa dear, there is such a peacefulness about you."

"I think the time has come to let the family know that I won't be here for much longer, don't you agree Charles?" she said.

Charles put his arm around her shoulders and, drawing her close to him, said, "Yes, I do Louisa. We both know how frail you are becoming. How shall we tell them?" he asked, dreading it.

"I think maybe tell Letty and Wilf later today, then tell our parents and Evangeline when they visit over the weekend," she suggested.

"I know it's not going to be easy, especially since Mother and Evangeline are arranging a family Christmas dinner in Lauder Road this year," Charles replied, "Oh Louisa, this is so unfair. This Christmas was to be a celebration of our family being together again, with Evangeline's change of direction in life and relations between us being so harmonious now," bemoaned Charles, "and you are not going to be well enough to enjoy it."

Louisa sat up and looked at Charles. She turned and took his hands in hers and said as gently as she could, "Charles dear, I am not going to be here at Christmas. It's not a matter of not being well enough to enjoy it, I simply won't be alive."

As her words sank in, Charles began to cry. He realised she was right and that he had been deluding himself that Louisa would make it to her favourite time of year. She'd always loved Christmas, with a child-like delight and excitement. He thought bitterly, that last Christmas was just that - her last Christmas ever. As he wept, thinking of this, Louisa tried to comfort him, stroking his strong hands with her now very thin ones and making soothing sounds.

Eventually he stopped crying, took a deep, shuddering breath and kissed Louisa's frail hand. He was more himself now and he smiled sadly, saying, "You are right Louisa, as you usually are. You're looking very tired my dear, let's get you home for your nap." He looked out over the Forth and noticed that dark clouds were forming and shutting out the sunshine of earlier and he shivered, feeling it was a bad omen.

"Thank you Charles, I think a nap would do me good, I'm usually much brighter afterwards."

LATER THAT AFTERNOON when Charles went into their bedroom to waken Louisa with her usual post-nap cup of tea, she was in such a deep sleep that he momentarily panicked. He put down the tray of tea things and, automatically, reached for her pulse. He breathed a sigh of relief as he felt the slow steady beat.

She woke up with him still holding her wrist and she said, "Charles? I was in such a deep sleep and dreaming about the three of us going cycling up to Blackford Hill," she said dreamily, "isn't that strange? That was years ago when Evangeline was a little girl on the tricycle my father gave her for her birthday."

"I know, dreams can be strange my dear," Charles replied gently, "Do you feel like a cup of tea? Maggie sent up some shortbread, it's still warm. Will you have a piece?"

"Just the tea, thank you Charles."

They sat in companionable silence as they drank their tea, then Louisa said, "Charles, I've been thinking about telling everyone and, I wonder, would you mind going and telling them? I don't feel that I have the energy for it," she said, "and I think it might be easier for them to hear it from you."

"Of course I will, Louisa. I'll go first thing tomorrow," he replied.

"Except Letty and Wilf," said Louisa, "Would you telephone them and ask them to come here this evening?"

"I'll go down and do that right away, hopefully they won't have a prior engagement."

THAT EVENING, Louisa made a monumental effort to get dressed, ready for their best friends' visit. They were in the drawing room when Letty and Wilf arrived after supper, when Louisa had eaten so little that Maggie had been upset, thinking Louisa hadn't liked what she'd cooked for them."

Charles, who'd had very little appetite himself, tried to smooth Maggie's ruffled feathers. "Your mistress is just feeling a little under the weather Maggie, the meal was delicious."

Maggie was unconvinced, as she pointedly looked at his plate and said, "But you havenae eaten much either, are you under the weather tae?"

He placated her by saying, "Maggie, you provided us with such a magnificent picnic that I'm afraid I rather over-indulged, so I didn't have room for much of your delicious meal this evening."

"That's a'right then," she said to Charles and, turning to Louisa, she said, "Ah hope ye're feelin' better soon Lady Frobisher."

Louisa smiled weakly and said, "Thank you Maggie."

"Are you remembering to have coffee ready for our guests later Maggie?" Charles asked.

"Of course, it'll be ready for eight o'clock Sir Charles."

When Maggie showed Letty and Wilf into the cosy drawing room, Letty was shocked at the change in Louisa, since she had last seen her friend just a few days before. She looked at Charles questioningly and he nodded.

Letty kissed Louisa's cheek while the men shook hands and she sat on the sofa next to her. Wilf sat on the sofa opposite, but Charles remained standing by the fireplace.

He cleared his throat and said, "I'm afraid Louisa and I have some very sad news ..." and he told them about Louisa not having a lot of time left.

Letty began to cry as she hugged her friend close and said, "Why didn't you tell me before now Louisa?" and she looked at her brother accusingly.

"Don't blame Charles Letty," said Louisa soothingly, "It was my wish that Charles and I had time to spend together, whilst I could still enjoy it, before telling the rest of the family," she smiled at Charles, love radiating from her face, "and we've been going for drives and having picnics."

Wilf spoke for the first time, "Louisa, I am so very sorry to hear this news, so very sorry that I can't put it into words." His voice trailed off and he looked miserable.

"I don't know how much time I have left," Louisa said, "but I now feel it's time to let the family know. Charles will tell my parents, Evangeline and your mother in the morning. Then we shall just take each day as it comes."

Letty looked at her sister-in-law with a mixture of astonishment and awe and said, "Louisa you are the most amazing woman I know and so courageous."

In an effort to lift the mood, Louisa said, "Let's have some coffee and some of Maggie's delicious shortbread, you know how offended she gets if you don't eat every piece."

Charles looked at his wife and smiled, thinking, 'That's my Louisa, rallying the troops."

47

EARLY DECEMBER 1913

As they had expected, Louisa's parents, Charles's mother and Evangeline had been devastated by the news of Louisa's impending death.

Louisa's parents in particular, could not come to terms with their daughter dying.

"It's not right Henry," wailed Emily, after Charles had left to impart the sad news to his mother and daughter. "One's children should not die before their parents. Why not me instead? I'm old, how I wish I could exchange places with our darling daughter." and she wept bitterly as Henry enfolded her in his arms, his own sad tears threatening to spill over. Both Henry and Emily, like Charles's mother, were in their eighties and still enjoyed good health.

EVANGELINE AND CHARLOTTE were overcome with grief when Charles told them and he was glad that his mother and daughter had each other for comfort.

Over the coming days there would be visits to Louisa from all members of the family and Charles tried to prepare himself for their sorrow, as well as his own, whilst taking care of Louisa.

Charles rejected Letty's idea of bringing in a nurse to help care for Louisa and between them they provided twenty-four hour care for her.

Maggie went around the house red-eyed and would not be consoled. She had adored her mistress and her master, to a lesser extent, since the time she had been rescued by them from the child white slave trade in 1885.

In the days following the announcement of the terminal nature of her condition, Louisa had become unable to get out of bed. She slept a lot of the time, but was able to appreciate the visits by the various members of her close family.

At the beginning of December, on one of Evangeline's frequent visits between lectures, Louisa was propped up on a mound of pillows and Evangeline was sitting by her mother's bedside holding her hand. She said, "Mother, I want to tell you that I am so sorry for all the worry I caused you during the years I was involved with the suffragettes, can you ever forgive me? I don't know if I can forgive myself." Tears ran down her cheeks.

"Hush Evangeline," whispered Louisa, "none of that matters now. You are going to be a wonderful doctor like your father and Aunt Letty. Women's suffrage is very important and you were acting on what you believed was right and I am so proud of you." This was one of the longest sentences that Louisa had uttered for days and she rested a while before continuing. "Evangeline, fetch my jewellery box from the dressing table please." Evangeline did as she was bid and brought the large velvet box to her mother's bedside.

"Open it," Louisa instructed, "and take out my wedding

and engagement rings. I want you to have them. Your father will sort out the rest in due course."

Evangeline was weeping quietly as she said, "Thank you Mother, I shall treasure them always."

"Now go back to your lectures Evangeline dear, I need to sleep now," whispered Louisa and she closed her eyes.

Evangeline kissed her mother on the forehead and said softly, "Goodbye Mother, I love you so," then she left her mother's bedroom to hurry back to the medical school and the remainder of the day's lectures.

LOUISA PASSED PEACEFULLY from this world on the morning of the fifth of December. Charles was lying, awake, by her side when he heard her speak. "What is it Louisa?" he asked, sitting up.

"Hold me Charles," she said, in a stronger voice than he'd heard in a while, "the light is fading now."

Charles put his arm around her thin body and drew her gently to him. He could see in the light of the bedside lamp that her, still beautiful, face had a translucent quality and he gently stroked her cheek and said, "It's alright Louisa, my darling girl, I'm here."

She sighed contentedly and then breathed her last breath. Charles looked at the clock and saw that it was ten minutes past six o'clock.

He sat there, cradling Louisa's body for a long time as her warmth faded, reluctant to let her go, knowing that this was the last time he would hold her in his arms.

Eventually, when he heard Maggie moving around in the kitchen, he laid Louisa gently back on the pillows. Letty would be arriving at seven and he realised he must have been holding Louisa for forty minutes.

He got up and dressed quickly, then went downstairs to break the news to Maggie and to await Letty's arrival. She would be the one to write the death certificate and he knew he would have to make the funeral arrangements, but he couldn't face that just yet.

Taking a deep breath and straightening his sagging shoulders, he went into the kitchen. When Letty arrived a little while later, she found Charles comforting an extremely distraught Maggie and she knew at once that Louisa was gone. She left the kitchen quietly and went upstairs to say a final farewell to her lifelong friend.

LOUISA'S funeral service took place on Friday the 12th of December at St Giles' Cathedral, where she and Charles had been married twenty-seven years earlier. The service was attended by over two hundred people who knew and respected Louisa personally and from her work with the police, as well as her service on the School Board. Colleagues and friends of Charles and the Moncrieffs and the Frobishers all gathered to pay their last respects.

There was a large contingent of women from the National Union of Women's Suffrage Societies and members from the Men's League for Women's Suffrage there also, to mourn the woman who had worked long and hard for women's suffrage. Many were heartbroken that she had died before women had been granted the vote.

At the front of the Cathedral sat the main mourners with heads bowed in sorrow. Charles looked a forlorn figure with his mother on one side and Evangeline on the other, with

Letty and Wilf next to her. At the other side of the aisle sat Louisa's heartbroken parents.

Louisa's coffin stood at the front of the church with a single spray of white lilies on top, which Evangeline could not take her eyes from. She found it impossible to believe that her lovely mother was lying, cold, inside it.

Prayers for the soul of Louisa were said and a eulogy was given by Dr Williamson, the minister of the Parish of St Giles. After the final hymn, "Abide with Me," was sung, Louisa's coffin was carried by six pallbearers and put into the waiting hearse to be taken to St Cuthbert's churchyard for internment in the Moncrieff family plot.

As her coffin was lowered into the ground, more prayers were said and Charles and Evangeline said a final goodbye. Amongst the graveside mourners were Rose Buchan, who had been especially fond of Louisa, and DCI Wilkie, now retired from the Edinburgh police force, along with the other close family members.

"Come Mother, Evangeline," said Charles and they made their way from the churchyard to the waiting cars to take the family and main mourners to Heriot Row, where tea and refreshments were being served.

Charles had wanted to go straight home to Hatton Place to be alone with his grief, but out of respect for Louisa's parents, he had agreed to go to their home and thank everyone for their condolences. "After all," he thought to himself, "I shall have the rest of my life to be alone in Hatton Place, without my darling Louisa."

48

IN CONCLUSION

In the weeks and months following Louisa's death Charles was inconsolable. He had taken to driving to the places he had visited with Louisa in the four good weeks she'd had after Professor Duncan had told her there was no more that could be done to stem the spread of her cancer. He got some consolation from sitting in the car where they had stopped for picnics and he would relive those days.

By the beginning of June 1914 he came to a decision. He would do something to be useful to society instead of moping around the house with Louisa's ghost. He knew that was the last thing she would have wanted him to do and he could hear her voice saying, "Come now Charles, enough is enough. It is time to make yourself useful."

He decided that he would do a refresher course in medicine and return to work as a doctor. Little did he know, at that time, that this was to change the course of his life, for a few years at least.

On the twenty-eight of June 1914, an event occurred that would push the world into a terrible war. The Austrian-

Hungarian Archduke Franz Ferdinand and his wife were assassinated in Sarajevo by Serbian nationalists and this was the catalyst which led to World War One.

Lord and Lady Moncrieff

Emily Moncrieff knew that she would never come to terms with her daughter's untimely death. However, she made an effort to keep working towards the goal of women's suffrage, as Louisa had asked her to do while she talked to her in the days before her death. Henry was just a shadow of his former self.

Evangeline

Evangeline still carried guilt over her mother's illness but after several conversations with her grandmother, she decided to channel what her grandmother regarded as a "useless emotion" into working hard for her degree in medicine.

She had already decided that, after completing her general training, she wanted to specialise in the diagnosis and treatment of cancer. She felt, in a strange kind of way, that she could make it up to her mother for the years of worry and stress that she had caused her.

Evangeline and Jessie dearly wanted to live together but Evangeline was reluctant to move out of Lauder Road and leave her grandmother on her own. The old lady, who could, by now, read her granddaughter's moods, and knew something was troubling her, spoke to Evangeline one Sunday after lunch.

"Evangeline dear, I know something is troubling you,

won't you tell me what it is? You never know, I just might be able to help."

"Actually, there is something Grammie, but I am reluctant to say, I don't want to upset you." She bit her lower lip, frowning and feeling she was in an impossible position. On the one hand, if she left her grandmother to live with Jessie, she would feel she was betraying the old lady, but, on the other hand, if she didn't move into a house with Jessie, she would risk losing her relationship with her best friend and lover. Jessie had found secretarial work at Edinburgh Royal Infirmary after leaving her employment as an organiser of the Women's Social and Political Union and they had planned on renting a house near the Meadows which would be very convenient for both Evangeline's lectures and Jessie's work.

"I have a suggestion to make to you Evangeline dear, and it just might be the solution to your problem, since you are clearly in the throes of some dilemma," Charlotte said.

Evangeline looked at her in surprise and wondered, "could my grandmother possibly know what I am struggling with?" but Charlotte interrupted her musings.

"I was thinking that this house is far too big for me on my own, or even for us both, and I wondered whether you might like to ask Jessie if she would like to come and stay here. After all, it would be more convenient than traipsing back and forth to Jessie's flat, now that she doesn't live above the office any longer. What do you think?"

"But Grammie ... but ..." stammered Evangeline, "you must be a mind reader, that's exactly what's been troubling me. Jessie and I would love to share a house but I didn't want to desert you, you've been so kind to me over the years," said Evangeline, smiling widely now.

"I might as well tell you this now Evangeline," said Charlotte, "I have willed this house to you and I'm not going to live forever. So, I thought, if you and Jessie didn't mind having an old lady in the house, why not live here?"

"Oh Grammie, thank you so very much, you don't know how much this means to me, to us," gushed Evangeline.

Charlotte smiled affectionately at her granddaughter and said, with a twinkle in her eye, "Actually Evangeline, I think I do and I hope you and Jessie will be very happy here and I have always been fond of Jessie, you know."

Charlotte Frobisher

CHARLES'S MOTHER, Charlotte, had always been a resilient woman and she was a tower of strength to Charles and Evangeline in the early weeks and months following Louisa's death. She missed her daughter-in-law and grieved for her privately, but her life was fuller and happier than she had thought it would be, with Evangeline and Jessie sharing the large house with her. and her loyal hound, Rosie, of course.

Letty

LETTY WOULD NEVER COMPLETELY GET over losing Louisa. They had been friends since they were at school and were more like sisters. However, she didn't want Wilf to worry so she tried to hide the worst of her grief and she knew that, with the passage of time, she would come to terms with her loss.

Maggie

MAGGIE WAS KEPT on as housekeeper to Charles, but the light had gone out of her life. She and Rose were reunited in their mutual grieving for Louisa and she joined Rose in the Women's Freedom League and became enthusiastic, for the first time in her life, about the female franchise.

The Women's Social and Political Union

WHEN WAR WAS DECLARED, Mrs Pankhurst ordered a cessation of militant activity and urged her members to get behind the government and work to become part of the war effort by doing the jobs that the men had done before being called up. In this way they worked in the previously all-male industries, including shipbuilding, making ammunition, driving buses and a plethora of jobs they had previously been kept out of.

An amnesty was declared and suffragettes still serving prison sentences were released and their sentences quashed.

THE END

GLOSSARY OF SCOTS WORDS AND PHRASES

- a' - all
- aboot - about
- Ah - I (first person singular)
- ain - own
- airms - arms
- ane - one
- an' - and
- a'thegither - altogether
- awfy - awful or awfully
- aye - yes
- ayeways - always
- bairn - child
- ben the hoose - into the house
- cannae - can't or cannot
- claes - clothes
- cauld - cold
- couldnae - couldn't or could not
- dae - do
- daein' - doing
- didnae - didn't or did not

- dinnae - don't or do not
- disnae - doesn't or does not
- doon - down
- efter - after
- fae - from
- feart - afraid
- gey - very or quite
- gie - give
- gie'n - given
- gon - going
- gonnae - going to
- hadnae - hadn't or had not
- hame - home
- havnae - haven't or have not
- hen - term of endearment (female)
- hoor - whore
- hoose - house
- intae - into
- isnae - isn't or is not
- jist - just
- ken - know
- laddie - boy
- laldy - as in "give them/it hell"
- lassie - girl or young woman
- ma - my
- Ma - mother
- mair - more
- masel' - myself
- nae - no
- nane - none
- naw - no
- o' - of
- oan - on

- ontae - onto
- oot - out
- polis - police
- sae - so
- shouldnae - shouldn't or should not
- tae - to or too
- tellt - told
- thae - those
- thegither - together
- the morn - tomorrow or tomorrow morning
- tholed or thole - suffer or endure
- wee - little or small
- wernae - weren't or were not
- wi - with
- wid - would
- widnae - wouldn't or would not
- wis - was
- wisnae - wasn't or was not
- withoot - without
- wummin - woman
- ye - you
- yer - your
- ye're - you're

ABOUT THE AUTHOR

This is Kay's sixth novel and the third, and final one, in the Frobisher Family Saga.

Born in Edinburgh in 1954, Kay was educated at St Thomas Aquinas Senior Secondary School. She left school at the age of sixteen to work in the Civil Service.

A decade later, as a young mother, she graduated from Edinburgh University with a Joint Honours Degree in Sociology and Social Policy. Her undergraduate dissertation led her on to postgraduate research into child abuse and neglect in nineteenth century Edinburgh.

Kay worked for many years as psychotherapist and counsellor, specialising in working with survivors of child sexual abuse and domestic violence. Retired now, she lives in rural Northumberland with her husband and two sight hounds, Poppet the whippet and, rescued greyhound, Bertie.

Visit her website at www.creaking-chair-books.com and on Twitter.com/KayRace2

ACKNOWLEDGMENTS

I would like to thank my husband, Keith Race, for the time and commitment he has contributed in editing the manuscript and making this a better book to read. His thoroughness and patience is very much appreciated.

My warm thanks also go to my friends and family who have encouraged and supported me on this journey, particularly Nell and Trish, in Connecticut, who are always interested in the progress of my books. Thanks also, to Marie Robertson, Sam Thomas, Anne McKay and Jim Divine for your continued support.

AFTERWORD

It was certainly a very long and hard-won battle for women to have the vote extended to them, stretching from the first mass petition presented to Parliament in 1866 (the first one, ever, was taken to parliament in 1832) until 1928, when all women were finally granted the right to vote. Of course, the franchise was given to women over the age of thirty in 1918.

This battle, for battle it was, was waged by thousands of women (and some men) in various suffrage organisations including, the Women's Freedom League, the Actress's Franchise League and many others. This book focuses mainly on the Women's Social and Political Union, although my previous novels explored the suffrage societies founded as early as the 1860's, who came together in 1897 under the umbrella of the National Union of Women's Suffrage Societies, and who had a membership in the region of 50,000 women.

In recent years there has been much media attention regarding the issue of violence against women and how endemic it is in the UK in the twenty-first century. Sadly this is not a new phenomenon since women have been under attack from men for centuries. It was so bad in Victorian and Edwardian times that women went in fear of being molested in the street - so much so, that many carried whips or batons to defend themselves when out and about.

The above refers to assaults by strangers, but the extent of violence against women in their own homes is unknown and it's likely that it was as prevalent as it is today, if not more so.

Then we come to the institutionalised violence that was perpetrated on the women who went on hunger strike in prisons, up and down the country. This, in many instances, also constituted sexual violence since some women were forcibly fed via the vagina or rectum, causing extensive internal damage and injury. Was this state-sanctioned rape?

The facts surrounding "Black Friday" demonstrate the length that Winston Churchill was prepared to go, to quash the right to be seen and heard.

Some members of the Liberal Government were so opposed to granting the vote to women that it leaves me wondering how long they would have been denied it had World War One not broken out. All militant activity ceased and women backed the war effort, not only being employed in traditional male-only occupations, but also serving as nurses near the front lines in France and Belgium.

The battle for equality is still being fought on many levels and in many aspects of life in our society today. I can only hope that, at some point in time, women and girls and men and boys will be treated equally, in all facets of life.

I can't help seeing similarities between the direct action used by the suffragettes in getting publicity for their cause and a demand for change, with those organisations today, such as "Stop Oil" and "Extinction Rebellion", whose members glue themselves to walls or lie down across motorways in protest. Another parallel is way the governments then, and now, are trying to crush people's right to protest. Indeed, the two most recent Home Secretaries have introduced legislation to make peaceful protest a criminal offence.

Kay Race

October 2022

Printed in Great Britain
by Amazon

10456690R00161